GOOD FENCES

To Dick + Clare,
Our special friends
at the lake!
I will always cherish
the memories we share!
Thank you,
Marshall Crane
July 2010

Published by: Shapato Publishing
PO Box 476
Everly, IA 51338

ISBN: 978-0-9821058-8-7

Library of Congress Control Number: 2010921589
Copyright © 2010 Shapato Publishing

All rights reserved. No part of this book may be reproduced or transmitted in any form or by any means, electronic or mechanical, including photocopying, recording, or by an information storage and retrieval system, without permission in writing from the publisher.

This story is a work of fiction. Any resemblance to real people is entirely coincidental.

First Printing February 2010

Cover art created by Greg Foreman

Pg. 209: *In the Desert* by Stephen Crane (1871 – 1900)

This novel is dedicated to all whose lives have touched mine in some small or great way; a part of you is in this story.

    Marshall Crane
    Spirit Lake, Iowa

GOOD FENCES

Marshall Crane

Shapato Publishing
Everly, Iowa

ONE

I woke with a gut-empty feeling. It happens when I think of those I have loved and lost. I was thinking about my father. He died years ago. Dad practiced law in a small town in Middle America, a tax and estate specialist. He was beloved in the community, and his charity toward others earned him much business. As a father he was a benevolent dictator, ruling hearth and home with an iron hand of fairness.

I'd loved him and I still missed him.

While tripping and tumbling through my high school years, Dad employed me to clean his office every Wednesday night. I earned fifty bucks a month, and I learned the meaning of a buck. The money was welcome, and there was a side benefit that came with the job. Wednesday night was church night in our little town. I was a teenager and didn't need God on Wednesdays and didn't go to church. My Presbyterian buddies were stuck in church thinking, *Shit, Rick Burns is cool.*

But back to my father.

He had a rather large office for a one-lawyer business. It was located on the second floor of a two-story building in the middle of a town filled with two-story buildings. Nineteen tiled steps rose up from the street entrance. I washed those nineteen steps once a week. At the top of the stairs, on the left hand, just inside the office door, lay a long and narrow waiting area with eight chairs and two tables mirrored in tight formation against each of two walls, reminding me of a sort of mini-courtroom waiting for the jury to take its place. A small room opposite the door housed a secretary and her desk. To the far left of the entrance, one of two office windows looked in on the head secretary and her desk. These two ladies were Dad's permanent employees. He employed a third and sometimes a fourth during tax season. These "temps" worked out of another room located to the right of the hall door. Two desks, a conference table with four chairs, several gray metal file cabinets and two walls of library shelves filled the space. The shelves held American Law Reviews, and in a special glassed-enclosed area, the state's Law Codes stood at attention, the first volume dating 1848, sequencing to the present. Open the glass front and there was the unmistakable ancient smell of dust and glue binding. The oldest volumes were fragile in their tan-jacketed antiquity.

Dad was proud of this collection of legal history. He once told me, "Son, in order to understand the law, one must understand the evolution of law-making. These codes trace that history. If you ever want to see how our state got to where it is today, read them."

Well, I never did.

Dad's private office door was within yelling distance of the head secretary with the second of the two office windows. A dark chocolate-colored leather couch sat directly under the window, its leather scent meeting each visitor as they came in for consultation. Two paintings hung on the wall; both represented different aspects of foxhounds making a chase through an English countryside with horses and riders in hot pursuit. Two heavy oak chairs parked themselves at a glass-topped mahogany business desk behind which "The Judge" operated from a high-backed tanned leather rocker.

I remember one night after cleaning, I was in a snooping mood. I sat in dad's chair and rolled it up to the desk. An ever-present ashtray sat on top, filled with the residue of packs of cigarettes, the rancid smell of mouth-wetted filters and many days' old tobacco cinders begging for disposal, but there were other important matters to attend to. I checked the lower right hand desk drawer and found a bottle of Glenkinchie Scotch whiskey, two glass tumblers and a carton of Old Gold cigarettes. Dad used to light one cigarette from the nearly spent burning ashes of another. I understood the cigarettes.

One day I asked him about the booze. He told me about Frank Horst.

Frank Horst lived on a Century Farm. Frank had looked into his mortality, and at age seventy-five didn't like what he saw. He wanted the farm to continue in the family after he died, so old Frank sought out Dad. Inheritance taxes could be avoided if the farm wasn't in old Frank's name. Dad prepared him to sign ownership of the family farm over to his boy, Frank, Jr.

Dad liked to talk in parables, and I often wondered where his stories were headed. I was wondering about this story.

Well, Frank, Jr. was a decent son, thirty-five years old, with a pretty wife and a little daughter, and he wanted to stay on the farm. The setup was perfect. The proper documents were readied and old Frank took pen in hand to sign the ownership succession. But instead of signing the document, he sat motionless at that mahogany desk, staring at the papers, hands sweating and shaking. He looked helplessly at my father. Old Frank was simply unable to give away control of the farm. Out came the Scotch and a conversation. An hour later old Frank worked up the courage to do the right thing.

Dad was a pretty smart lawyer. He knew people. This isn't a learned trait; it's part of the DNA. He knew his Scotch, too. I wondered if I had gleaned a scrap of his genetic map.

One time Dad stepped out of his comfort zone when asked to work with the defense team on a criminal trial case. He had worked criminal cases when he'd been County Attorney thirty years before, and admitted he missed the thrill that went along with trial work.

At stake in this particular case was the future of a teenage boy who was being sued for negligent homicide by the parents of a girl who'd died as a result of an auto accident. The boy had been the driver. The dead girl, his girlfriend. The two were coming home together from a ball game one night. There was a head-on crash at the crest of a hill. Someone had crossed the center line. The trial lasted four days. When the jury finished deliberations, Dad called home and asked if I wanted to come to the courthouse to sit in on the announcement of the verdict.

It was tense in the courtroom. Families on both sides feared what could take place. Dad and his partner had bet on which jury member would be chosen foreman. Lawyers do that. It seemed a bizarre diversion at a time like this. After about twenty minutes the jury came back. The verdict, "Not guilty."

The boy's parents were ecstatic. They cried for joy. Their son smiled in relief and he cried, too. The defense lawyers smiled stoically, and I smiled because my father had won the case. But the dead girl's parents? They cried too. They were left alone a second time—the first by the accident, this time by the law of reasonable doubt.

The boy had probably been at fault, but no one could be certain.

Less than a year later, on a summer evening, along the same road where that accident had occurred, this same young man was driving home from work. It was a balmy night. His windows were down to catch the winds off the road. A fully loaded lumber truck he was following let loose a piece of two-by-four-inch pine. The last thing the kid probably saw was that board crashing through his windshield. It sliced his head from his body.

My father never did criminal work again, and he never talked about that boy.

Three years later, Dad gave up his ghost to cancer. A tumor lodged first in his left lung, and surgeons removed part of it. Then the cancer started on his right lung. The surgeons revisited and the chase was on. The cancer decided to go to the brain, detouring first through the lower back for good measure. The surgeons gave up. It wasn't sweet and it wasn't quick . . . not quick like a two-by-four.

The day after Dad's funeral I went to his office, and in the lower right hand drawer of the mahogany desk found seven packs of Old Golds and a half bottle of twelve-year Scotch. I damned the cigarettes to hell and drank the Scotch to empty. But the booze didn't give me the courage to do the right thing when I would sorely need it twenty years later.

Well, anyway, after that, a young lawyer bought my father's business. This young guy worked hard to maintain the practice and keep the clients, and he was successful.

Two years later and a week before Christmas, following a

twelve-hour workday, this lawyer closed shop for the night. He was the last out of the office. The secretaries, in the spirit of the season, had purchased a Christmas tree from the local Kiwanis Club and set it in the waiting room, lighting it with colored bulbs.

After flicking off the ceiling lights and crossing the threshold of the office, half in and half out of the room, the lawyer noted that the tree was still lit. As he later told the investigators, he looked at the tree and thought of his wife and their new son and the gifts under his own tree at home, and decided, for the sake of the season, to leave the lights on. He locked the door, walked down the nineteen tiled steps to the street below and happily headed home, whistling "Jingle Bells."

Back up in the darkened office the tree shined for, well, nobody, really. Its nettles had thirsted for water, the lights were old, the wiring frail, and the resulting fire engulfed the entire building, destroying everything: my old man's desk, his high-backed leather chair, the historical state codes for which he had taken such pride. All gone . . . along with any tangible grasp I had of the business side of my father.

What kind of karma does that to a man's memory?

TWO

I was nineteen when my father died. I wanted to be like him. I gave three years to his memory through government and literature studies, until I realized that the practice of law was not my calling. Something in me felt that karma and two-by-four pine boards would be the final judges on most issues. So, instead of a juris doctorate, I walked out of the University of Colorado with a teacher's certificate and a job in Estes Park.

For the past twenty years I've taught literature to seniors: Shakespeare and Dickens, Steinbeck and Hemingway, Robert Burns, Frost and Wordsworth. It's been a mildly fulfilling career.

I've never married. The thought of loving someone "Till a' the seas gang dry" seems a bit too long. Even punishing.

I am not opposed to love, for the sake of love, by definition. It's worthy of study. I've been in love. It used me. It hurt me. I stay away from love. I teach about it for the sake of the paycheck. And that's okay.

Estes Park is a nice town. The rushing sounds of the Big Thompson and Fall River are a constant wherever you walk. Born at twelve thousand feet, they run their courses into Estes Park. Their confluence comes at midtown, becoming then the Big Thompson River. It flows on to Loveland, which lies thirty miles east on US 34 and three thousand vertical feet down from Estes Valley. The Twin Owls, a rock formation to the north, keeps sentinel watch over the river, Lake Estes, and the people of the village.

Estes Park is a resort town which owes much to the tourism dollar. And like other resort towns, a diverse population calls it home. There are some old-timers who sit in coffee shops in the early mornings. They don't embrace diversity. They see diversity as the breakdown of society. They see that diversity changes the way we are and the way we will be. Some grab onto that idea and take it all the way to the grave. I once read somewhere that old men often "confuse their private terminal sensations with that of universal twilight."

I think the town will survive this debate. In fact, embracing diversity might be what actually saves society in the end. But, what the hell do I know?

Estes Park abuts Rocky Mountain National Park, and every fall elk herds take over the city when they come down from the high country to mate in the valleys. At night the city park is home to females and their yearlings. During the day, elk graze the back yards of homes, fairways of golf courses and just about anywhere they are allowed to roam. The elk walk through town in the predawn hours, helping themselves to human food sniffed out of trash receptacles set up along the sidewalks on Elkhorn Avenue. If you rise early, you can go up into Rocky Mountain National Park in any number of valleys and watch the sunrise show. As if on cue, elk herds appear from out the pine and aspen groves, onto the open valley floors. Here bulls seek dominance and rack-to-rack meetings with other bulls. Their piercing call fills the valleys with dreamlike echoes.

The bulls, in want of cows to add to their harem, separate potential mates from an established herd into the new herd, all the while running and dodging and hiding, waiting for the right moment to stake a new female, their ghost breaths exhaling from nostrils in the crisp cold mountain mornings. It is a sight.

It's beautiful here in Colorado. It's close to perfect. I'll love it till I die, if I live that long.

THREE

"Mr. Burns?"

"Jan," I said, deadpanning.

"Mr. Burns. Can I go to my locker?"

"'*May* I go to my locker, Mr. Burns'. . . and yes you can."

There you have it. This is teaching. Life is complete. Take me now, Lord.

"Sorry. *Ma-a-ay* I?"

I nodded.

"Thanks, Mr. Burns."

Jan would be back in five minutes, right at the bell. Jan was blonde and attractive, intelligent, and didn't smack her gum while chewing. I appreciated her more than she'd ever know. Gum-smackers drive me to distraction. And Jan was predictable. So were they all predictable.

At some point in this chosen career my attitude toward teaching took a slightly negative turn. I liked the kids, and they demonstrated a respect for their teacher in a sort of hands-offish way. But there was something that lessened my actual desire to teach as time went by. Perhaps it was not caring enough, or maybe it was an awakening that comes to some after years in the occupation. Yet it wasn't really the kids that caused this attitude. It had much to do with the society of education itself.

In spite of all the research spouted by the education noblesse, we never really seem to improve upon that which makes us human learners. Education leaders insist that the human being can be improved, and they insist that teachers center their classroom instruction on that predicate. As appealing as it sounds, there is a flaw in this ideal.

Toward this end education modifies and recycles itself about every seven years. Each cycle creates a new vocabulary to learn, new paperwork to complete, new theories to explore, new research to discuss and the testing . . . oh, the testing of applications to determine what makes a new and improved human being. Those poor politicians and theorists continue to believe that man can be taught into a better being.

It really wasn't so complicated: We are what we are. We all have brains which learn at certain capacities. As we age, the brain changes. Cells rearrange themselves, synapses close rank (or not). There is nothing teachers or well-meaning politicians can do to either improve on it, or, thankfully, destroy it. This is the human process. This is biology. It's been this way since Adam and Eve. Since that first fish stood up on two legs.

Abraham Lincoln was a self-made man who learned under the most primitive of physical circumstances. Had he lived today, in this technical world of ours, he would still be the same man, neither any better nor any worse. I have seen little to suggest that we have improved on Abraham Lincoln. Perhaps he could have had better timing in his choice of theatrical performances.

I tired of working through education cycles. Show me a way to improve on the Gettysburg Address and find a human being new and improved over Lincoln. Then we'll talk.

What I have with these kids is this: They know me and I know them, and we get along fairly well. There's no excessive pain on either side. I merely help them adjust to their evolving capacities and challenge that capacity. That's what a good teacher and education itself should aim toward. Some teachers do perform better than others, granted. But we try to leave no one behind.

"So, Pip loves Estella with a passion, but she does not return the favor. Who is responsible for Estella's obvious lack of good taste?" I asked no one in particular.

The class went into evasive action. Some sweated, others shook, and still others slunk down into their seats or ducked behind either their laptops or the person directly in front. They didn't like the question. All of them except Josh Holston, who sat in the back corner, staring at nothing, saying nothing and reacting to nobody. I didn't call on him, and that was okay. Josh was nineteen years old, old by senior standards, which may account for his silence in class. I sensed he would graduate quietly and disappear into the future, quietly.

Josh Holston moved in from Mississippi last year, but he never had any crowd to hang with in school. Again, his age may have been a factor. His hazel eyes reflected little of his thoughts and I'd never really seen him smile. He did, however, demonstrate a level of intelligence that separated him from the ordinary. He made choices from angles the rest of us didn't always understand. When he contributed, he challenged me in ways other students did not.

Josh looked, in all respects, normal. He stood five-foot-eightish with brown, close-cut hair and a diamond stud earring sparkled from his lower left ear lobe. Fifteen pounds overweight, he was like many other slightly overweight students. Josh dressed like other kids. Today he wore a brownish western-style shirt, the kind with pearl snap buttons, Levi jeans and Tony Lama boots.

A native to Estes Park, Josh's father came back to work hardware in a store on Route 7, south of downtown. His mother was a dental secretary in a practice out on Highland Drive. The family appeared to have settled into Estes Park comfortably. Whatever baggage Josh brought with him to school was secreted away somewhere. None asked and none seemed to care. He was a cipher in the mountain snow . . . a large cipher, a deep snow. There were lots of Joshes in this beat up world. They needed attention but did not often get it. I didn't give Josh attention.

Well, no one wanted to address the question of the moment. It was old Miss Havisham who turned young Estella into a man-eater. She took them by their hearts, tore them up, and spat them out. I knew this. I had lived this. But did Marcus Jermot? He played football and dated Jan. He was a slinker.

"Marcus, sit up! What do you think about Estella?"

Marcus pushed his linebacker frame halfway into position. He'd been watching the sway of Jan's hips as she walked out of the room, his mind no more on *Great Expectations* than mine was on whether or not he knew the answer.

"Who, me?" he asked.

Marcus chose his words wisely and infrequently.

"Yes, Marcus. Do you see any other Marcus in this room?"

Brilliant. I had Marcus right where I wanted him. It was like shooting fish in a barrel.

"Uh, what was the question, Mr. Burns?"

Ah, I was ready for that, too. But Jan spoiled it all by walking back in the room, her hair still blonde, jaw working on Trident, hips swaying, and everyone looking her way. The bell rang.

Marcus, I thought, *I'll get you next week*. He saw my look. He knew he would be "on the rack" come Monday.

The students filtered out of the room

"Good-bye, Mr. Burns."

"Bye, Amy. Have a great weekend."

"See you, Mr. Burns."

"Monday, Evermore . . . " I pointed my index finger at him.

"Yah, okay," he laughed. "Hey, Mr. Burns, it was Miss Havisham who taught Estella to be a man-eater, right?"

"Atta boy, Bob. Stick with that story."

He laughed out the door. Bob Evermore and Amy Crenshaw were good kids.

It was the weekend, middle of May, one week till summer break, and the kids' minds nestled on spring baseball and track. For myself, I had a Mazda MX5 outside in the parking lot, waiting for me to pop its top and test the curves up in the National Park, a ride I took as often as possible.

"Rick!"

Damn!

Sue Richy came walking down the hallway from her classroom. Sue was a fellow teacher. She taught accounting and coached girls' track. She was an attractive woman, soft blue eyes and skin to match, high cheekbones and a proud stature. Sue had the look you see in pictures of ancient Egyptian queens, long and elegant, tall and slender. Auburn hair fell to her shoulders. She was wearing a blue cotton boat-necked Gap sweater which hung easily outside straight-legged jeans above Nike runners. It all fit her well, like a catalog picture. Sue had the body of an athlete, a four-hundred-meter hurdler who'd represented the University of Alabama at the summer Olympic tryouts eight years earlier. She was single and eight years my junior and I was not interested except as a critical observer. She wanted someone to help her with field events. I knew this. I had other plans.

"Hi Sue. Say, I have a four o'clock appointment with Steve Shields, insurance stuff, you know," I lied. "Can't make it tonight."

"It's alright," she said. "I actually came to tell you that Dan and Maggie are here to help out with high jump and discus, and the shot-putters are working on technique with Shirley. Don't need you tonight. Take care. Have a great weekend. My best to Steve, Mr. Burns."

She was heavy on the "mister." That was sarcasm.

Sue waved, turned and walked away.

I watched her go through the side door, opening on to the track. She had a nice sway to her hips. Interesting. But, shit, never waste a lie if you can help it.

Hell, now I had to talk to Steve about weaving tangled webs.

FOUR

Slipping behind the wheel of a Mazda MX5 comes with ease, if you're five-foot-five and weigh 150 pounds. I touch on six feet and tip out at 215. So, it's butt first and legs close behind. The fit was snug and that's just fine by me. The leather seats accepted my weight and the six-speed manual was poised. A turbo-charged engine, with high octane in its belly, itched to take the familiar, high winding road to Deer Ridge Junction and on to Trail Ridge Road.

Running to 12,000 feet on Highway 34, Trail Ridge Road was the highest continuous road in the U.S. It passed the continental divide and fell down on its windward side to Grand Lake, a quiet and peaceful village, a little more removed from the madding crowd that was Estes Park.

The winter snows had been above normal by Colorado standards and the road was closed at the nine thousand-foot level. The two snowplows especially created for these mountain roads and their drivers were both a little outgunned by wet spring snowfalls. The goal was to open by Memorial Day. It might not be until the first week of June that Trail Ridge would be completely opened this year.

The afternoon sun was working to get to 65 degrees, but this car would be open-aired in a few seconds. I unhooked the two fasteners on either side of the windshield, released and lifted the black cloth top over my head to rest behind the front seats into the roof well. The engine had a starting sound that awakened the kid in me, a low rumbling soft purr at 900 rpms. There was no hurry. I clutched into first gear to 10 mph, second to 20 and out the school parking lot. I avoided looking straight on at the practicing track team, but the peripheral eye caught a waving Sue Richy (shit), and I moved third gear to 30, fourth to 45, past the Stanley Hotel on my right, fifth to 60, the engine hitting 3,500 rpms. Sixth gear would release the tension on the engine, but I wanted to keep tension there, for later use on the uphill curves ahead. Toyo racing tires hugged the middle of the road along 34, Fall River cutting through the mountains on the left, below the road, and rock cliffs rising on my right. The Miata stayed to the road like a train on the track. Inertia pushed me to the side at the curves; my confidence in this car was a proven.

The air was just this side of too cool, even with my green long-sleeved shirt. I had an Old Navy dark blue sweatshirt in the trunk of my car. It was an old thing, shredded at the cuffs and around the collar, but the sleeves were long, and it had been with me for ten years. I stopped the car and retrieved the sweatshirt. It fit loosely and comfortably over my frame.

Rocky Mountain National Park, past Fall River Entrance, lay ahead. The anticipation of the drive gave way to a mental and physical release of tensions, which was important to the male of the species. It was a good escape.

I drove to the first overlook of Horseshoe Park, and moved to the curb, settling in neatly between white-painted parking stripes. I enjoyed coming up here. From this vantage point I watched for Rocky Mountain sheep that come down from higher up to graze the grasses and drink from Sheep Lakes. These lakes, ponds actually, contained mineral salts that the sheep desired. They needed to come down to the valley for this water. I kept a pair of Bushnell 10 x 24 binoculars in my glove box for such occasions, to get up close and personal for the show.

It was already colder here than in Estes Park. I had come up about fifteen hundred feet in altitude from the school. I grabbed my gray Early Winters stocking hat. Its Gore-Tex kept the head warm. The hat was fifteen years older than my sweater and was made in the USA. Imagine that.

I was the only soul parked at the overlook. I kept the engine at idle, allowing the turbo to cool off before shutting down. There wasn't much time before the sun disappeared over the peaks, but there was time to enjoy what remained of the day. I looked out at the mountains: Mummy Range to the northwest; Mounts Chapin and Chiquita; Ypsilon Mountain rising to thirteen thousand feet. I turned my eyes to the valley below and shut the ignition. The silence was sudden and nearly alarming. The scene was worthy of Bierstadt's brush strokes. As majestic as the mountains were, the valley below, with Fall River swinging lazily through grasses before its plunge toward sea level, was equally awe-inspiring.

I got out of the car and held the glass prisms for a view. Over toward the ponds and up the mountainside there was no activity yet. There was no guarantee the sheep would show simply because I was there to observe. They worked to their own will, not mine. One needed to appreciate that about Nature. Her theater opened on its own timetable, at times when we most expect it, at times rarely, or not at all. And herein was the beauty, when you are haply there to witness.

Not everybody approached the mountains as they should be approached, which is slowly.

Last summer on the Bear Lake hiking trail I'd run into a visiting family. They were going at a brisk pace, and it was obvious the father was in a rush to see as much of the scenery as possible in as short a time as he could work it. They plowed ahead on the trail around the lake, below Hallett Peak and Flattop Mountain. They were all hurry, hurry, hurry. He saw me. He was huffing and wheezing. I was sitting on a large boulder that reached out into the north end of Bear Lake, soaking up sun.

He'd wheezed and asked, "Is there anything on ahead?"

I looked at him a little longer than was necessary and replied, "Well, have you seen anything yet, buddy?"

"Asshole," he'd spat/wheezed, and off they went, circling the lake, like clowns running round a circus ring.

Mountains take time . . . and shallow breathing.

FIVE

Darkness came, and so did the cold, but not the sheep. I went back to the car. The top went back up, and I started the engine, turned the heater to low but didn't leave the parking lot. I sat and thought. When I sat and thought, my mind sometimes became undisciplined and wandered to places I didn't want to visit. But whenever I caught myself doing that, it was already too late.

That place was Sara Reese. It was an old hurt. It was from a long time ago, from the days when my heart still leapt up at rainbows in the sky.

Sara had come to Colorado by way of San Diego. From my country boy point of view, she was The Beach Boys' California Girl in the flesh: straight blonde, waist-length hair on a five-foot nine-inch frame, supported by long and perfectly shaped legs. Her eyes were emerald green, lips promising, and her breasts invited attention. Sara's presence commanded the scene wherever she happened to be. Guys and gals alike looked to her for acceptance and she fed on the attention.

Sara was a drama and music major at CU. I was the lawyer wannabe. I had a sense of humor and unquestioned good looks, of course. And I obeyed. Where she went, I went. When she dined, I dined, when she slept, I slept with her. Watching her move and listening to her sing sent my soul to heaven. Loving her was drama itself. I watched her on stage. And at every curtain rise I fell in love with her all over again—Sandy in *Grease*, Desdemona in *Othello*, and Laurey in *Oklahoma!* I fell in love with her, curtain call after curtain call.

Our lovemaking was gentle and fierce. Obviously it came time to marry this woman. The ring was purchased, the proposal made, the irony followed.

Sara wanted to experience it all. Rick Burns was a part, a bit part as it turned out, on her road to fame. Sara Reese had doors to open. And that meant some doors would close. I stood behind just such a closing door, in an empty room, watching the light from the other side fade away from me, narrower and narrower the light, till there was only a sliver of Sara remaining, till there was nothing. And I was alone, in the dark, holding a ring and a broken heart.

As every man will tell you, when your heart is broken you go to your car and drive. I drove to Central City to gamble and drink beer. I was as true as my word. I gambled. I drank beer. The ring exited my car around 10:30 that night somewhere along Route 279, just outside Central City. A few minutes down the road I discovered I was not finished with the drinking. I found myself in the Black Forest Inn, testing the quality of German ales. The bartender and I decided on Reissdorf Kolsch. It was smooth. So was the waiter's accordion rendition of "Edelweiss." Everything after midnight that night was a blur, including the ride back to Boulder.

Sara Reese was the first woman I'd ever loved. The memory of her lives and breathes in the pit of me, surfaces when I find myself alone and wandering, whenever a timber loosens in the fence I built around me after she left long ago, whenever I fool myself with thoughts of peace.

Shit. Double shit.

SIX

My cell phone broke the scene. It was a relief, really. I picked it up, checked the caller ID, and said, "Hey Steve."

"Rick!"

"Yes I am, buddy"

"Rick, where are you?"

There was urgency in his voice, not usual for my insurance man.

"I'm up in the Park. What's wrong?"

"Okay, you need to get back to town now. Something has happened, and Jesus H. Christ, it's bad! Jesus!"

"Slow down, Steve," I said. "What's happened?"

"Just get to my office."

"Hold on a minute." I tossed my phone onto the passenger seat, shifted to reverse, backed out of the parking lot and raced the gears to six toward Estes Park. I picked up the phone and continued with Steve.

"Now, buddy, what is going on here?"

"When will you get here?"

"I'm driving through Horseshoe Valley as we speak. Give me a few minutes."

"Shit . . ." he said, and the connection broke off.

Steve was a good friend and too young a widower made. Her name had been Debbie. She'd been a wonderful blonde-haired, blue-eyed woman. They were married ten years ago in Jamaica at the Half Moon Resort near Montego Bay. I was the best man, standing beside a very nervous insurance agent under a cabana at the end of a peninsular arm of land stretching into the Caribbean Sea, as we watched Debbie walk on air down the path toward her lover and husband-to-be. It'd been a fine time, a happy time. They'd settled in Estes Park till death did they part.

Three years ago Debbie drove down to Denver for a meeting of the Young Democrats. After the meeting, while driving back to Estes Park, she'd stopped the car to call Steve. She didn't know where she was on the road. She knew she was going home but couldn't remember how to get there. This was a road Debbie knew blindfolded. Steve had her stay where she was and drove I-25 till he found her.

She was scared. She had reason to be. It was a tumor, a fast-growing and terrible tumor. Three weeks later, Debbie died. Steve clung to me and I supported him.

Until this phone call, I hadn't sensed him so upset since that day he watched his wife lose her short battle with Mr. Death.

It was this urgency in his voice that made me understand a bad thing had happened.

Steve's office was in a small suite of rooms in a log-framed two-story building set next to the Pizza Hut by the city green space, right off Alpine Street. It was nearly dark when I got there. His Tahoe was parked in front. The window in his office was the only light coming from the building. Town traffic was not heavy yet. It was early in the season. In two weeks Elkhorn Avenue would be a mess.

I hurried inside the building. His office was a comfortable room, done up in Bob Timberlake fashion with painted hangings of mountain themes on the pine walls and large overstuffed red-brown leather chairs on either side of Steve's desk, his own chair a rocker throne. The floors were wood floors. Real wood; man wood. Steve was not sitting. He was pacing, but he was not alone. Sue Richy was there, and when I came in the room, her eyes reached out to me. They were water-reddened and she looked completely broken. Steve saw me at the same time. I didn't know who to comfort first because Steve was as broken as Sue.

"Steve," I said. "What the hell is happening?"

"Rick, there's . . . there's . . . uh . . . oh, shit. There are two dead kids. Amy Crenshaw and Bob Evermore. Josh Holston killed them. He shot them. They're dead, Rick. I was there. I saw it all."

"Oh," I said half dazed, looking about the room for Bob and Amy to jump out and yell Gotcha! They didn't. "I mean . . . what? Where?"

"Over at Dempsy's." Steve's voice was full of anger and fear and desperation.

Dempsy's is a convenience store/gas station east of town, at the corner of Saddle Road and 34. It was a hangout for the kids, after school and on weekends.

"Where's Josh?"

"The cops have him. He was sitting on the curb by the entrance to Dempsy's. He used a shotgun. He was sitting there, with earphones on, listening to some iPod shit. Rick, he blew the faces off those kids and then he went and sat on the curb like it was Sunday at the playground. I was in the store when it happened, but thank God Tim Cavern was there."

Tim Cavern was a part-time deputy with Larimer County. He was reliable, young and a credit to his town. I worked with Tim during the summers. We were both part-timers with the police department.

"Tim was pumping gas when the Crenshaw gal and Evermore drove up to the store." Here Steve broke into the story Tim shared with police and confirmed by Steve and other witnesses. "The Holston kid was sitting in his car off to the side of the store. You know how kids park down there and just sit and talk with friends? He was sitting there like any normal kid, but when that gal and Evermore got out of their car, Holston got out of his car. Cavern said he watched the nut kid walk up toward Amy. She was closest to Holston. That's when Tim saw that Josh was holding something along his side and then he saw it was a shotgun, and Holston raised the gun as he neared Amy. She didn't even see him till she turned away from the car toward the front of the store. She was face-to-face with the nut, and he shot her in the head. He blew her head off!

"I was standing at the check-out and I saw it. Cavern fell to the ground behind his pick-up, slid over to the back of the truck bed and looked up in time to see Holston aim the gun toward

Evermore. Evermore turned away and went down to the ground. It was all slow motion, Rick. Holston walked around the front of Bob's Chevy, adjusted his aim, and shot Evermore in the back of the head. That poor kid's face . . . all over the parking lot.

"Cavern was like thirty feet away and he didn't have his gun with him he told me later, but he had his cell phone and he called Jim Harris at the station. After the call, Tim looked over to see where Holston was. That's when he saw him sitting on the curb of the walkway right by the front door, the shotgun lying next to him while he adjusted his earphones. Tim ran around his truck and threw himself into Holston like a Bronco linebacker. Some of us who were inside the store and closest to the door, ran out and helped Tim hold Holston down while he grabbed the shotgun. But there was no fight in the crazy son-of-a-bitch."

I was dazed. "Anyone else hurt?"

Steve looked to Sue and back to me, shaking his head. "Uh, no, I don't think so."

I turned to Sue. "Are you okay?"

"Oh, Rick," she said. And with that Sue, who had sat down while Steve told the story, rose, put her arms around me, pushed her face into my shoulder and wept.

At the moment I had two free arms with no place to go. So, I held Sue. She seemed small and fragile. But when she brought her face away from my shoulder, there was a questioning look in her eyes.

"Why, Rick? Why didn't we see this coming? What do we not know about kids like Josh until it's too late?"

"I don't know, Sue." I turned to Steve. "What else happened?"

"Well." Steve sat down, leaning forward at his desk, elbows on top. "Jim Harris got there within five minutes. Tim had called the ambulance and they were there a few minutes after Jim. Jim cuffed Holston, spoke briefly with Tim, and looked at the scene in front of him. He read Holston his rights and took him to jail. The department was in full mode by then. More cars came and the area was secured. Those of us there gave our home addresses and phone numbers and were told to go. We were told that statements would be taken later. That's when I went back to my office and called you."

I turned to Sue. "How did you get here?"

"I was working with the runners at track and Jennie Brens' cell phone rang. It was her mother. She was at Dempsey's when it happened. I remembered you said you were going to Steve's and I called the office. He told me you were on your way."

I sat down and breathed deeply, head in my hands. Sue and Steve consoled.

My mind swam with thoughts of two-by-four pine boards and Scotch Whiskey and the total lack of good sense to do what I knew I should have done. Josh Holston needed help a long time ago. I'd paid him no attention, and why? Because I'd lacked the moral courage to extend myself to him. This was part of the answer Sue was searching for.

And it was a terrible truth.

"Anything of Josh's would be confiscated," I said. "Computer, cell phones, notebooks, diary, clothing—any sign that would predicate violence. Jim will have all that in hand by now. You and I can offer our assistance. We're two teachers who've known Josh and we should know these kids as well as anyone. Josh's parents might not be in any shape to help. Maybe we can offer somewhat objective eyes."

"It makes sense, Rick," she said.

"Do you still want to come?" I asked.

"Yes . . . sure."

I wanted to ask her why, because I sensed there was something more she wanted to say.

The sheriff's office was less than a block away, so we walked. It was a silent walk. There'd be no good in what we might find. It was a quiet and thoughtful walk.

Jim Harris was a good cop who had worked for the state patrol for fifteen years. He'd paid his dues out on the highways and byways of Colorado. He spent ten years on I-25 between Fort Collins and Colorado Springs. His last stop as a highway patrolman was a caravan of in-transit cars, speeding their way south. He stopped the group north of Denver. Jim clocked them on radar at high speeds. He threw his lights on as the first car, a Cadillac, was within range of sight. The whole crew pulled over. There were seven vehicles, all Cadillacs, Fleetwood models, large and fast and all white.

Jim called the stop in to dispatch right away, and moved to the first vehicle. The window came down and, as Jim leaned to the driver, a .357 Magnum greeted him with a blast to the chest.

Jim was knocked across the road and into the median. He never saw the cars leave the scene.

Luckily, Jim had been one of the first law officers to wear the new Honeywell GoldFlex body armor. It was a type II-rated armor, thinner and more resistant then Kevlar, and rated to take a .357 Magnum bullet. The jacket proved its worth that day, but the Colorado State patrol hadn't prepared for Diane Harris, Jim's wife of twenty years. She had waited for her husband to come home every night for the last fifteen of those twenty years. When she received the call on her husband, he

SEVEN

I looked at Sue.

She seemed to read my mind. "Rick, there's nothing we can do now. It's done. The kids need us now. Superintendent Rowles was on the radio and called all teachers to school tomorrow morning. He'll open up the doors to the community."

"It's a good idea. It's the right thing to do, but right now I want to go to the chief's office," I said, getting up and heading for the door.

"Wait, Rick. May I come along?" Sue had placed herself between me and the door. Her eyes were red and her hair pulled back and knotted. Her face was determined. There was no arguing the point.

"Okay."

We looked at Steve.

"I have to call company headquarters," he said. "I hold insurance policies for the Evermore family. That's why I came here first. Herb Evermore had a small policy taken out on Bob. It was a policy meant to serve as a savings account till Bob reached eighteen. The policy was then convertible to cash for college. There was a life benefit attached in case something happened. These things are just not meant to be. Damn!" He reached for his phone.

I opened the office door, and Sue and I left.

Outside, the streets were dark and the lights showed shadowy. I looked at Sue, trying to see into her eyes.

"I need to find out why," I said.

"Alright, Rick," she said. She was looking at me and I hoped she couldn't see the utter hopelessness I felt, the guilt and shame.

was in an ambulance, and she was on the way, with intent.

Jim woke up in St. Anthony Central Hospital in Denver with one hell of a sore chest and Diane by his side. He submitted his resignation the next day, was heralded a hero and went into local affairs in Estes Park, along with Diane and their son, Zach, both living a more secure life with a chief of police for husband and father.

Two days after that shooting, fourteen elderly men were found by hikers, tied and gagged and locked in an old miner's cabin about five miles off I-25 up by Fort Collins. The men had been driving the Cadillacs to auction in Denver from Sheridan, Wyoming when they stopped at a rest area. A black man approached the lead driver, put a gun to his backside and other black men came up to the other drivers. They were put into the cars and taken to the cabin, tied and gagged. Ten empty husks of Cadillac Fleetwoods were discovered three weeks later on an empty dirt road near Nogales, Arizona. And that was that.

Sue and I saw Jim through the window of his office and walked in. Jim looked up and showed us a tired face. To him, we were two more questions to answer to and he was not taking questions.

"Hello, Jim." My weak attempt at innocent conversation.

"Rick... Sue. What can I do for you? I'm very busy. This is a real mess."

Jim's office was Spartan. His desk was an old oak teachers' style with a drawer in the middle and three deep pull-out drawers on either side of the chair well. His chair was an oak rocker set on four roller coasters with a butt pillow covering the seat. On the top sat a Dell Inspiron and a John Deere coffee cup filled with pens and pencils. A printer sat on a tray table abutting his desk, papers strewn across its surface. A square card table sat against the north wall and on it was a black ten-cup Krups coffee maker, its decanter half empty with what appeared to be very black coffee. A Folgers tin and a tower of white Styrofoam cups sat next to the maker. A couple of spoons lay by a stack of napkins and packets of sugar and creamers filled a green plastic order-out basket. Jim held a Styrofoam cup in his right hand.

"Jim," I said, "I'll get right to the point. Sue and I want to help you in any way we can."

He looked at us with no particular interest.

"We know these kids," I continued. "Amy, Bob and Josh have been in our classrooms. We've learned something about them. If there's any clue as to why this happened, we might catch it somewhere in the children's personal effects."

I looked at Jim and his face relaxed a microfiber.

"Okay," he said. "I didn't want you here when I saw you come in. Sorry Rick . . . maybe you can help. I don't mean to sound ungracious. You've been a good deputy for me during the summers when it gets hectic around here. You were a big help when it came to dealing with the kids uptown or out in the county. I remember that time we had to break up a little beer party in Glen Haven. There were over 150 kids there. You talked with a few of them, and what could have been a messy situation with kids running all over hell to escape arrest, because of you, turned out to be a rather peaceful walk-away. I owe you. Plus, you know how the system works."

He sighed, and looked at the mess of papers spread across his desk.

"We have the kids' computers and cell phones in the back room of the station," he went on. "They're tagged, hooked up, charged up and ready to go. I can appoint you and Sue as examiners under my supervision, and you could begin to try and connect the dots."

"Has Josh said anything?" I asked.

He shook his head. "Not a word. He hasn't said anything to anybody. He's closed down completely. We have him in a holding cell with the standard twenty-four-hour suicide watch to be safe. It's routine."

Sue looked away and wept quietly. There was nothing gratifying about any of this mess. Two lives lost and three families pretty much destroyed, and sitting in a jail cell, the one who could give answers but wouldn't. Maybe Josh simply couldn't give the answers we all needed to hear.

"Okay, we'll get busy." I looked at Sue. She nodded. "If there's an Internet link among the three, we'll find it," I said.

"Sue, let's check personal web sites, blogging history, e-mail, music and video downloads."

Jim actually looked relieved. "Thanks, you two. Write down whatever looks suspicious, mark it and we'll review it when you're finished. I'll take you to the screening room."

EIGHT

He rose and led us out into the hallway, turned right, and at the third door stopped, reached into his pocket for a key, and opened the door.

"We need to keep the chain of evidence in order," he said. "The computers are locked in to us and only we or those appointed by us, with supervision, can have access to them. So, Phil here will be with you at all times."

"Hi, Phil," I said, lifting a hand in greeting. "Haven't seen you around for a while."

Jim said, "I'll be in my office working on reports. Good luck to you two." He turned and walked back down the hallway.

Phil led us to the room along a darkened hallway lit by a single, bared 60-watt bulb.

Phil was a former student at Estes Park, having graduated three years earlier, and he'd entered the Colorado Law Enforcement Training Academy in Spring Valley as soon as he turned twenty-one. His dad had been a retired copper who'd worked security for Brinks and was killed in an armed robbery attempt when Phil was eighteen years old. The tragedy put Phil and his mother into becoming self-providers. It was difficult, but they'd survived. Phil had come back to Estes Park to be with his mom and his friends.

"Hi, Mr. Burns. Hey, Miss Richy," he said. "I feel terrible for what happened. I mean, it's just like I never thought anything like this would happen here. Stuff like this happens in other places . . ." His voice faded away.

"I only wish, Phil," I said.

Sue said, "How's your mom, Phil?"

"Oh, Mom's fine. It's been kinda tough. That first year was

hard on both of us. Mom gets out and works full time now down at Wranglers Clothier, ya know. She really likes it there."

Phil unlocked the door and we went into the screening room. It was a barren room with a long table and two chairs. On the table were three computers, each marked with the names of the three kids.

Phil said, "I'll be right outside the door if you need me."

Sue and I looked at one another. Without a word, we sat at the table. I had Josh's and Bob's computers, Sue had Amy's. Finding the passwords proved to be easy. Passwords are usually written down on paper found in the general area of the computers. We found Amy's and Bob's passwords taped to the backs of their computers. Josh's was taped under his keyboard.

We began to cross-reference any link that might bring the lives of these kids onto common ground. The work was tedious. Amy's interests lay in Abercrombie and Fitch, Bob's in sports, and Josh's in hunting.

Their cell phones showed no cross-reference to one another, no twittering and no shared contacts. In fact, Josh had no contact list at all.

We worked into the night hours but found no evidence of communication between any two or among the three.

Amy and Bob were dating, so there was the obvious linkage there, but with respect to Josh and Amy and Bob . . . nothing. No e-mails and no blog sharing, no Facebook entries and no messaging. Not a hint to show these three had any communication of any sort, nor for that matter, even any similar likes or dislikes.

Josh's e-mails were limited. He had no real friends and his mailbox showed that, but there was nothing Sue or I deemed suspicious.

God, was this a random act, a killing for sport? There must have been intent on the part of Holston. He'd meant to kill. It'd been premeditated. He'd had the gun. But had he intended on targeting just Bob and Amy? Were they random? Like when a young kid takes his twenty-two out to shoot at birds. His intent is to shoot birds, but no birds in particular, only those birds that are nearby and convenient to his position. Is that what

Holston had done? How does one define those intentions? But most important, why? Why kill two people like they were birds? And why these two? It defied reason, and Josh Holston wasn't speaking.

Sue looked to me. "Rick, I don't know where to go from here. It's like chasing a shadow. His mind works at a level I don't understand."

That's when something clicked in me. I recalled a brief conversation I'd had with Josh one day a few weeks ago. I had asked him about a paper that was due the following week, and he'd said to me something like, "Finished tasks need finishing, right Mr. Burns?"

"Right, Josh," I'd said. I remembered thinking that this was not a clear-headed response to the inquiry.

Now, the way he'd said the phrase, "Finished tasks need finishing," sounded almost like a philosophical exclamation.

"Sue, I have an idea. Stay with me a minute will you?"

She moved beside me and looked over my shoulder.

I typed, "Finished tasks need finishing," and clicked search.

Up popped ten million responses. This was no good. So I deep-webbed, "Philosophy, finished tasks need finishing," and up came something I certainly had not expected.

NINE

"What is that?" asked Sue.

"I really don't know for sure."

On the screen were the words "Finished Tasks Need Finishing, The New World Order," printed in large red lettering on a black background. Dripping in red were tears of blood beneath the lower-case letters "i" in the words "finished" and "finishing."

There was no other link on the page. No audio, no other words showed on the screen, just this.

I went back and entered, "Finished tasks need finishing, The New World Order," adding to it and entering these other words: blood, dripping, school, kill, guns, black, red, power, bible, demons, books, hate, and murder. Nothing came up that would lead us to anything worthwhile.

"I need to talk with Josh Holston," I said.

Sue looked at me. "But he's not talking, Rick."

"He'll talk sometime. And he may talk with me."

I got up. Sue was close behind.

Outside the door, Phil was sitting in a folding chair, reading *The Rocky Mountain News.* He folded the paper, then stood, straightening his shirt. "Can I help you?"

"I believe we're finished here, Phil," I told him.

"Okay. I'll have to stay with the computers."

I nodded. "Thanks. You take care of yourself. Say 'hi' to your mom for us."

"Will do, Mr. Burns." And with that Phil opened the door and disappeared back into the room we'd just vacated.

Sue and I found Jim in his office, working on a press report for the morning paper.

"Jim," I said, "I may have found something interesting."

He looked from Sue to me, resting his hands on the desktop. "What?"

"As far as making a connection between Holston and either Evermore or Crenshaw, there is nothing. Except that he killed them. As for coming closer to answering the question of why he did it, there may be a chance." I explained the search on Holston's computer.

"I want to talk with Josh to see if there's some connection with this 'finished tasks' thing," I said. "How is it with him?"

"He isn't talking to anybody from this office or the CBI or the ATF," said Jim. "I believe he's crazy, but like a fox. He's a nut, Rick. But he's a sane nut, and we will crack him. Let me show you something."

Jim stood up and went to a door in the corner of his office. He reached into his pocket and pulled out a key. He opened the door. Behind it was a storage room, containing shelves and wall hooks. There were many items stored in that room, including guns and rifles and ammunition of all types and sizes.

"This is where we store evidence," Jim said. "All the items here have been marked and, where needed, dusted for prints." He reached up to a shelf and pulled down a shotgun. "This is the weapon Holston used on Bob Evermore and Amy Crenshaw."

He held the weapon at the stock in one hand and at the pump handle with the other. He turned and faced us.

"It's a Winchester Super X3, 12-gauge Cantilever deer shotgun, with a twenty-two inch barrel. It's a killer instrument. Take a good look at it. This is what Holston used. This is how he took it up to his shoulder."

And with that, Jim brought the shotgun up to firing position quickly, aiming at the far wall of the small room.

"He fired it, first at Amy and then at Bob."

He took the gun down and put it back on the shelf, sighing a tired man's sigh. We left the storage room. He locked the door again.

"You look at this, Rick, and you have to think that whoever would do something like this is crazy. I don't think he's crazy."

"So, Jim," I said, "it really makes me wonder. Why do perfectly sane people do completely insane acts?"

Jim looked at me and said, "That's the $64,000 question. His parents came while you and Sue were working in the screening room. They're good people. They are so devastated by what their son has done that they can't even talk about it yet. Josh won't speak to them, either. You're welcome to try. What we need to find out is if this kid worked independently or if he's in cahoots with someone else. If there is someone else involved, we need to find out fast and move on it. If you have a hunch that he'll talk to you, let's go with it. Wait here."

Jim disappeared to the jailing quarters.

Sue and I sat and waited. We didn't speak. We were each lost in our own thoughts.

Jim was away maybe five minutes. When he came back he said with some disbelief, "Josh wants to talk with you, Rick."

I stood up.

"Sue, you probably had better stay here," said Jim. "It seemed pretty clear Josh would see only Mr. Burns."

"Sure," she said. "I'll sit here and wait." But she didn't look happy about it. Sitting and waiting were not in her vocabulary. She looked at me. "Be careful, and good luck."

I took a deep breath and followed Jim to the jail block.

He took out a handful of keys and used one to open the first door, a heavy metal one with a thick nine-by-nine inch window at head height. Inside there were two separate cell areas. Each was about eight-by-twelve with your typical jail bed (steel springs on four legs with a thin mat on top) and toilet (no lid). No loose impediments lay about that a desperate inmate could use as a weapon against another or himself.

I had a passing thought of Andy of Mayberry, Otis, and Barney Fife, and I did take a quick glance between the cells, looking for the easily accessible ring of keys hanging on a nail. Dumb nerves on my part.

Josh was in the north cell. The other was empty. He was sitting on the bed with his arms crossed, leaning back against the wall. He turned when Jim and I came in.

TEN

Jim led me to the north cell, pulled out an old wooden four-legged chair, placed it before the bars, turned to me and said," I'll be just outside in the next room if you need anything." His voice echoed in the room.

I said, "Okay, thanks." And out he went.

Up to this point I had not made eye contact with Josh, but I could feel his eyes on me. I took in a deep breath, turned to face him head-on.

Except for the bars separating us and the mere fact that this young man had just killed, in cold blood, two of his classmates, Josh looked like any high school kid.

"Hi, Josh."

"Hey, Mr. Burns. How ya doin'?"

Oh, this was just fine. I'm the teacher and he's asking the questions.

"Josh. This is not a 'How ya doin'?' kind of day. You understand that don't you?"

"Yah, I do. That Miss Havisham was a real bitch, wasn't she Mr. Burns? She really screwed up Estella."

It was as if he had no sense of what he had done.

"Josh. You shot and killed Amy and Bob this afternoon over at Dempsey's. You know that, right?"

"Yah, I know."

This was getting us nowhere fast. Josh was still looking at me with a nonchalant gaze.

Then he said, "Phil Banders graduated a couple of years ago didn't he? His dad is dead."

I turned to look for Phil, but he wasn't near.

"Yes, his dad is dead. He lives with his mother."

Why were we having this conversation? This kid needed focus.

"Josh!" I said sharply. He looked me straight in the eye. "Why, Josh?"

He turned away and looked toward the only window in the cell. He was quiet. It was eerily silent but for our mutual breathings in and out.

I finally took the chance and said, "Finished tasks need finishing, Josh?"

"Something like that, Mr. Burns." He turned and looked at me, a Mona Lisa smile playing across his lips.

"Josh, you've killed two people with a shotgun and you aren't saying why. All I know is you won't talk to anybody else, but you will talk to me. Why talk with me?"

Josh was quiet. He stared at me. Was this a contest? If I read his mind, I would win? He scanned me head to foot and smiled. I could tell Josh was thinking about what he should tell me and how much he should tell me.

This mental combat went on for another minute and he said, "Mr. Burns?"

"Yes, Josh." I was not going to like this.

"It's finished, Mr. Burns." With that, he crossed his arms, leaning back against the wall of the cell and was quiet.

"Josh? You were going to tell me something. Listen, here I am. There is a reason why you were willing to see me. You know the reason. There must be a reason for that. There needs to be a reason for all of this. Jesus Christ, boy! Talk to me!"

Josh Holston retreated inside himself. It was obvious he was through talking. I tried making eye contact, but he was staring vacantly at the cell wall. There was no more interest in eye contact.

I went to the outer door and knocked. Jim was there immediately. I walked out and to his office with him. Sue was there, looking rather haggard but eyes alert for what I had to say. I sat on the chair next to Sue. Jim took his seat behind his desk.

"What's up, Rick?" he asked. He poured coffee. I took a cup and sipped; it was hot and it was as strong as it had looked earlier. And I didn't feel well.

"There isn't much to tell you, Jim." I looked back and forth between him and Sue. "He rambled a bit, not seemingly interested, I made a comment about 'Finished tasks needing finishing' and he acknowledged that statement as if it had some meaning to him. I pursued that course and he clammed up, refusing to say anything more. That's it."

Jim sighed. "That's not much, but I didn't expect much." He looked at the walls of his office, a kind of cell itself, with Jim a prisoner in it. "Thanks, Rick. And Sue, thank you, too. You tried. No one is asking for more than that. You can sure feel free to pursue that finished tasks thing. It might connect to this."

Jim rose and walked around his desk toward the outside door, opening it. "You two go home. It's late. Or rather, it's early."

I looked at my watch. It was 4:30. I'd had no idea Sue and I had been here since early the evening before. All of a sudden, I was beat.

Sue and I left Jim and the jail. We walked back to Steve's office, our lungs filled with the cold contagionous night air of death and sadness.

We didn't say much. It was all quite overwhelming, and we still had to be at school in a few hours. Psychologists and counselors and ministers would be there. Many kids would stay home with parents, many others would come to be with friends and share the grief and ask "Why?" We had to be there to tell them that we just didn't know why. There would be tears shed on both sides, and we still won't know why. Only one person knew, and he wasn't talking. He was "finished."

Steve's office was dark and his Tahoe was gone. I took Sue by her left elbow and opened the door to her VW, guiding her into the driver's seat. She didn't offer resistance, but put her right hand on my arm and sat down, keeping the door open, one leg in and one leg out as she looked up at me.

I leaned on the door frame, looking over the top and down at her.

"Rick, we need to be strong for the kids, but I don't feel very strong," she said.

Gazing at Sue, the interior light of the car and a faint streetlight casting shadows over her face, I saw a beautiful woman with strength of character. Her eyes caught mine and held them. She was giving me the courage I didn't feel I had.

I said, "You'll be just fine. The kids respect and admire you. There's nothing you could say that would be wrong in their eyes. We'll get through this together, along with the rest of the staff. It'll come and it'll pass. Twenty-four hours in a day, as they say. By this time tonight there might be more answers than it appears there are now. Maybe Holston will talk."

Her eyes held mine. "And maybe he won't. Then where will it all end?"

"I'm not done with this, Sue," I said. "There's something I feel about that phrase Holston recognized when I said to him, 'Finished tasks need finishing.' There's more to it than what we think and than what he was willing to talk about."

"I hope so," she said.

I pushed the door in slowly as she got behind the wheel, started the engine and closed the door.

As I walked away from her car and over to mine, Sue rolled the window down.

"Rick, thanks for being there tonight," she called. "I didn't know what to do yesterday when it happened. You were the first one I thought of. I needed to see you right away. I don't know why." She attempted a smile. It didn't work. "I mean . . . well, thanks again."

She backed the VW up into an empty street and the side window went back up. The car rolled away, its engine purring and echoing toward Lake Estes and her home. I watched as the red taillights finally disappeared on Highway 34.

The street was quiet. The sun would be up in an hour. Emptiness filled my gut, and I looked at the Miata and the street and at the shadows of the mountains to the west which would soon be washed in pinks and lavenders. I sighed and my mind wandered.

ELEVEN

When kids die, school is a proper place to mourn. Schools brought most people together anyway. I went to the gym where staff and ministers and counselors gathered to be available to students who wished to be near to or talk with or vent out or whatever needed to be done to get through this time and to move forward. This place where basketball, wrestling, volleyball and PE classes were the order of the day, where yelling and cheering and action on the court or on the mats were ritual, where applause and admiration, post-victory celebration and post-loss commiserating were the glue that kept the community together. Now the raftered ceiling echoed the quiet sobbing of girls and reflected the silent gazes of somber young men and a gathering sympathetic public, testing the community glue in this gymnasium-turned-grieving-ground.

Superintendent Rowles spoke briefly. He announced that the double funeral of Amy and Bob would be held at Rocky Mountain Community Church the following Tuesday. He also announced the cancellation of the final four days of the school semester.

Several students came up to me, crying. This was a time when it was okay for teachers to have physical contact with students. There were hugs and hands lifted to shoulders, the kind of contact humans need in order to escape the numbness of what had happened, to feel connected, to share the grief.

There was anger. The boys in particular were angry with Josh. However, even this anger was short-lived and turned to quiet desperation through vacant stares looking for answers.

Some students grouped together in corners of the gym. Some wanted to go to classrooms or the commons area where they took their daily meals. Familiar places. Some wandered the building. We remained behind, giving them their space.

Toward midday, a few teachers approached those students who might have been able to shed some light on Josh Holston and his motives.

Their answers were all the same: No way did anyone see this coming. Sure Josh was a loner, but he had wanted it that way. Josh wasn't bullied, nor was he a bully. He was just scary to the kids. He had always kept to himself since he'd come here last year, sharing nothing and shunning those who attempted friendship, but never really mean-spirited toward any one. They all had sensed, though, an underlying potential for danger from Josh. We'd all sensed that. I had, too, but had done nothing about it.

By the middle of the afternoon most students had exhausted their grief and need for adult communion. What was left for them was to go home. And they went home, and it was over.

TWELVE

So Josh wasn't talking, and there seemed to be no motive to fall back on, except that I had a nagging idea that finished tasks needed finishing. It was a brick wall of frustration.

Josh's parents were equally baffled. Jim had questioned them Saturday morning at their home.

Sid and Mary Holston were decent people. They had always accepted their son as he was and they'd loved him. They could no more explain why Josh did this than any one else. Josh had always been a loner, even in Mississippi. But he had never been in any trouble. These two were so overwhelmed with grief for the two dead children, their families left behind and their own son that Jim saw no good in questioning them further.

Josh was arraigned Monday, prosecutors asking for the death penalty on two counts of first degree murder. His court-appointed attorneys pleaded "not guilty" for him, requesting bail and immediate suicide watch with psychological observation. Josh remained silent. He had clammed up completely. The judge held Josh without bail and set a trial date. Josh was allowed transfer to the Denver County Jail for personal safety stipulations as the wheels of justice began to turn.

The funeral was large. The church held 300 people. There were at least that many and more who stood outside and listened to the service over a temporarily arranged PA system. The teachers sat together for the most part: Maggie Potts, Shirley Delaney, Dan Green, Sue and me. Steve sat with us. The town pretty much closed down for the day. The Evermores and Crenshaws looked old and tired as they watched the caskets of their children being rolled down the aisle from the front of the church, to the hearse, to the cemetery. It was a difficult good-bye.

"Rick," Steve said as we walked to our cars, "what's the sense? Two kids are dead, a third kid is in jail. What's going on in schools today? I know this didn't happen in the school, but it just as easily could have. They're children. Violence in schools—Jesus H. Christ!"

I rested my hand on Steve's shoulder. "Something about our society lends itself to allow this kind of thing to happen. Easy access to weapons, opportunity, motive, television, video games, movies, clothes, style, culture, too much freedom, bad parenting, bad friends, hormones, bad teaching, bullying, being picked on . . . the list just goes on and on my friend."

Steve looked away as though I didn't given the answer he'd wanted to hear.

"Look, buddy," I said. I turned to him and made him look me in the eyes. "Debbie was a wonderful lady. There was no sense to her dying either. She was murdered, in a way, just like these kids. The cancer attacked her in an uncompromising way. All you could do was watch and wait for it to end. And we were left with the same questions. Maybe different answers sure, but you were thinking of Debbie when you asked me these questions. The hopelessness of the situation is beyond attaching an acceptable cause or reason."

Steve looked at me. For a second I thought he was going to bop me one on the nose because he stiffened as soon as I mentioned Debbie's name. But then he relaxed, breathed deeply and said, "You're right. I see these things happen and it irks me to no end. Then I think of Debbie. I loved her so much. I still love her."

THIRTEEN

I had to get away from people for a while, so I went home. I lived two miles outside of Estes Park on Highway 66. Just past the Dunraven Inn was a dirt road that disappeared into pines and rocks. I had a small log cabin I'd bought ten years ago. It was a fixer-upper. Pine on the exterior and pine on the interior and a green metal roof, because the contractor said it had a fifty-year guarantee. It was big enough for one, a thousand square feet. My needs were Spartan. When I'd started looking for a home I'd wanted to buy a cave but none were for sale. I'd been disappointed.

Then I'd found this treasure. Outside there is a separate one-car garage, a small front porch with two Adirondack chairs and a pinewood table with ashtray and tools for cigar smoking. I'm not a true aficionado, but I do appreciate a good Macanudo.

Occasionally I light up, get down with a good book and, depending on the mood, enjoy a glass of wine. Lately Chateau St. Michelle has been my little friend from the great state of Washington. I finished my last bottle four days ago. I made a mental note of that. If a visitor happens along to engage in conversation, the book goes, a glass of wine and a freshly cut cigar are proffered for their examination and use.

Inside is a living, dining, and kitchen area combined under a beamed ceiling and a real stone fireplace. I still enjoy the carrying of oak and aspen logs, the challenge of lighting the perfect fire, the smell of burning wood, and the warmth of the stones on cold and snowy evenings. The floors are wood planked with throw rugs set at different areas for convenience. Two Italian leather pieces of furniture compliment the living area, a three-person couch, and an overstuffed reading chair with a reading lamp off to the side. A rotating fan hangs from the peak of the ceiling.

On one wall is a seven tiered library shelf filled with books. The top two shelves hold books I've read twice or more: mysteries, biographies and histories. The next three shelves hold once-read books. The last two shelves hold a diverse assortment of literature, from a King James Bible to a Rand McNally road atlas that I update yearly, and a Spanish-to-English dictionary. I put older books on those shelves.

I have an old Latin text from university days, which includes Homer's *Iliad* (in Latin). I kept it because I'd never quite translated the entire story to the satisfaction of my instructor. That still bothered me. Although the instructor had been dead for ten years and wouldn't remember me even if she were living, I intended to finish the translation some day. The book needed dusting. Other texts included a seventy-five year old edition of *The American Pocket Medical Dictionary*, a *Birds of Colorado* pictorial, the complete, *Annotated and Unabridged Sherlock Holmes*, and other equally fascinating titles. The rest of the shelving was empty. I have work to do.

A Charles Russell print hangs on a wall opposite the books—cowboys on horses herding runaway cattle, which is about the only action going on in this house.

Beneath the print is a work desk that has just enough space for a laptop and my Bose wave sound system. A forty-two inch LED television sits in the corner, away from the fireplace. The oak dining table is round and bare, four matching oak chairs keeping it company. A sitting counter with two stools marks the start of the kitchen with its rock-tiled floor and gray slate countertops, black sink, black fridge, black-faced dishwasher and black stove/microwave combo. Not much room in the kitchen for more than one. Off the living area is a bath and bedroom with a queen bed. The artwork on these walls follows the western theme. Another Russell and a Remington, more horses and grassy vistas and washed out desert arroyos and cattle. In the back of the house are a workroom with washer/dryer and a door leading to an open concrete slab with a Holland grill for cooking, and just beyond that a path to my neighborhood, which is Rocky Mountain National Park.

With the day fresh in mind, I looked for something to fill the time. I did not want the mind to wander. I randomly picked a book from the top shelf of my library: *Coming of Age in Mississippi*. Oh, this would make a person feel better. If you ever thought life was dealing you bad cards, read this. When you finish, if you are white, two things might stay with you. You might just hate your white self and you might hate the human race in general; at which point you had better stop the complaining. If you were black, you might have wondered how this information was left out of American history books. There was despair out there you don't want to experience first hand.

I put the book back on the shelf, not because I didn't want to read it again, but because it reminded me of another book I had that I did want to see. It was on the lower shelf. I found it nestled between *The Complete Works of Shakespeare* and *Silas Marner*. Though a small book, the title suggested so much more: *Hate Groups of America*.

I'd done a paper for a graduate class a few years back, and I used this booklet for a quote about white supremacy groups operating in Idaho. The booklet was dated by eight years. I recalled that most of the racist groups listed in it were shut down, their leaders in jail for various crimes, from illegal arms to propaganda that incited both violence and racial intolerance. Most of these groups cited God as authority for justification of their despicable actions. Some memory about this book set up a red flag in my mind. And something else bothered me, but I couldn't quite put my finger on it. I took the book to my reading chair, turned on the reading lamp, plumped down onto the leather cushion and opened it up to the table of contents. The chapters were listed by hate group names. I thumbed down the listings and, toward the middle, there it was.

FOURTEEN

Page twenty-two, "FTNF." I turned to page twenty-two for a synopsis of the group: "A privatized militia; break-off from the Ku Klux Klan; comprised of civil rights revisionists; based in Mississippi; dedicates racist rhetoric toward bringing disorder through threatened violence and terrorism."

Ain't free speech grand?

I read: "FTNF is not well organized; members scattered and number probably less than one hundred. Manson (Mac) Jones and Terrence (Terry) Sims of Greenwood, Mississippi are last known principals of FTNF."

FTNF . . . Finished Tasks Need Finishing. Jumping Jesus!

I got up and paced the floor. What to do? What to do? This revelation required thinking food. Eating has always been my response to stress and revelation, and I went to the fridge. In it was a griller steak marinating in mango chutney. A baked potato and mushrooms, basted in butter and covered with sea salt, were wrapped in aluminum foil and ready for the grill.

Damn, FTNF! Where would this lead me?

One hour for the potato and mushrooms and fifteen minutes for the steak, a lettuce salad for starters. A bottle of wine, Black Swan merlot (thank you Australia), a full-bodied cigar—a Cuba Aliados—and quiet time to think. But there would be no peace in this.

FTNF. What was the connection between this hate group and Josh Holston?

I walked to the back patio and lit the grill, using a steel brush to clean off the charred remains of burgers and brats from last week when Steve had been over. He'd brought the beer, Dripping Moose. Steve thought he was funny. So did the beer's makers, as it turned out. We switched to Blue Moon before too long. It was the correct light ale for my taste on that night.

With a glass of Black Swan in one hand and the grill tongs in the other, I stood there, staring at the covered top. I wished the potatoes done, but a watched pot never boils. I did know that I felt a strong desire to find out what had happened to Josh Holston's head. He'd done a terrible thing, and I sincerely felt that, had I taken the time with him that I should have, Bob and Amy would be alive. I absorbed guilt fully and completely. I would find out why.

My stomach began to turn on itself. I tried to ignore it, but finally realized that as long as my stomach kept rumbling I'd be distracted from more important things.

I sipped the wine, dry with a hint of fruit. It would go well with a rare steak. The lettuce salad was mixed with shredded cheese, cherry tomatoes and Italian dressing, Wishbone is the best. Then the steak went on the hot grill. I moved the potato and mushrooms to one side, devoting an entire side to the meat and a continual rub of chutney as it cooked.

I drained the wine and poured another glass before taking the meal from the grill to the sitting counter at the kitchen. Heinz 57 on the meat and real butter for the potato brought it all together.

I picked up the TV remote and switched to the Weather Channel, proof positive that we Americans are obsessed with weather news. *Local on the 8s* was fascinating. The weather changed every six hours. What was "rain tomorrow" at the four o'clock break could become "sunny tomorrow" by the ten o'clock break. We humans always want to be the first to know and the first to share this information with the world.

The co-hosts of the show were a man and a woman, both too attractive for me to take seriously.

"Sure is cold out," the female announcer stated with complete self-assurance. "They say it'll snow."

Already tired of these two, I began to create dialogue in my head: "Yes, ninety percent chance tonight, but a sixty percent chance the snow will gradually turn over to rain with a seventy percent chance the rain will total from one quarter to one half inch by tomorrow night," from the male half of the duo, watching as she melted to submission.

The weather champion!

I turned off the TV.

The meal was first rate, but my nerves were jumping with thoughts of what it was I knew was coming. I wanted to put it off. I felt like a kid in a school speech class who had to give a speech and had avoided it as long as possible, but the teacher said, "It's time."

FTNF was waiting and it would not be put off.

FIFTEEN

With dishes soaking in the sink, cigar clipped and lit, I powered up the Bose and flipped in a CD. It was *The Buena Vista Social Club*, the Cuban experience. I didn't understand the language but life's rhythms flowed freely through the harmonies and soft strings of guitar and piano. This was thinking music, and I needed to think with a clear mind.

I sat in the wooden Adirondack on the front porch, ashtray on the table, within arm's reach, the Aliados nestled in a marriage of the right forefinger and middle finger balancing the cigar over the thumb. A small smoke trail rose and Black Swan swished the interior glass in my left hand, with music playing softly from the house.

There was a connection with Josh Holston and FTNF. Of that I was certain. FTNF was a racist organization, which makes a stereotypical kind of sense in Mississippi. The history of Mississippi includes the likes of those who hate all that is different from them. FTNF and groups like it thrived there, and I was certain they recruited and operated outside state boundaries. But what was it about this particular group that would attract a boy like Holston? How and why would he tap in to FTNF? There were no easy answers.

I looked at the definition of FTNF. "A racist organization bringing disorder through violence . . ."

Racist . . . racist . . . violence . . . racist! Holy Shit! I laid the cigar down and reached for my cell phone and punched Sue Richy's number.

SIXTEEN

She picked up on the first ring. "Hello?"

"Sue," I said, "this is Rick."

"Oh . . . hi, Rick. It's been a long day hasn't it?"

"Yah, uh . . . Sue, I'm sorry. I don't mean to sound in a hurry, but can you come over to my place, now? I have something to show you."

"Sure," she said. "Be there in fifteen minutes."

No questions asked. She was a good kid. But Sue Richy was no kid.

"Thanks." I rang off.

I went to the kitchen, put the cigar out under the sink faucet and put the dishes in the dishwasher. I went into the bathroom to mask the cigar breath with Crest gel. The face looked reasonably presentable, the red Woolrich long-sleeve was sufficient. Jeans and Lands' End moccasins completed the outfit.

I went out into the living room and looked at the fireplace, filled with wood and ready for fire, thought about it, but decided against it. What am I thinking? A fire isn't necessary and besides, a fire brings with it other things.

"Rick, you dumb shit," I said out loud to myself.

I heard Sue's VW come around the bend in the drive and went out to greet her. She parked next to the black Miata and got out. She was wearing hiking shoes, jeans and a dark green turtleneck sweater. The coming night would be cool. I noted that Sue's sweater color matched the color of her VW.

She walked up to the porch, her face smiling and questioning at the same time.

"Thanks for coming over," I said. "Wine?"

"Well, you are very welcome, Mr. Burns," she said. "Wine sounds good." She took the glass from me and took a sip.

"There's something I found," I said. "I think you would want to see it, and then there's something I want you to tell me after you see it."

"This sounds a bit cryptic. I like cryptic."

I retrieved the *Hate Groups of America* book from the porch table and gave it to her.

"Please, have a seat," I said, pointing to the chairs on the porch. Sue sat down with the book, curiosity in her eyes. I half sat, half stood against the porch railing opposite her. "This is a reference book I used a few years back when taking a Human Relations course for continuing education," I explained. "I wrote a paper about hate groups in Idaho."

Sue was giving me her full attention.

"Would you turn to the table of contents and tell me if you see anything interesting?"

"Okay," she said. She put the wineglass on the table and opened the book to the front. She began to read the titles. After a bit she said, "Page twenty-two looks interesting." And without my asking, she turned to the page and read the synopsis. Then she read it a second time. She looked up at me. "Rick, is this the 'Finished Tasks Need Finishing' that Josh Holston reacted to at the jail last Friday night?"

"Yes. I think it is. Now . . ." At this point I looked directly at Sue. "Tell me something else that makes sense out of all this."

Sue looked at the synopsis again for a few minutes. Then her mouth opened in shocked surprise as it hit her. She looked up at me again. "We've taught these kids for a lot of years, haven't we?"

"Yes," I agreed.

"And we see them grow and cultivate relationships with one another. Boyfriend, girlfriend, on again off again. Some stay together, some even get married. Most don't work out."

"Did we ever question Bob and Amy's relationship?" I asked.

"No," she said. "They were a good couple. They were good friends and had a strong relationship. We even thought that they might stay together after high school because they seemed such a good match."

I knew Sue was there, but I needed her to say what I thought.

I asked, "And what do you think now?"

"It never passed my thought processes Rick, because those two had gone together for three years and had come through the same school system together. After a while, when you know someone, you become blind to it."

Just say it, Sue, I thought.

"This act by Josh begins to make a perverted kind of sense now, after reading this," she said as she lifted the book to me and finished, "because Amy was white and Bob was black."

SEVENTEEN

I needed validation. Sue gave it.

We looked hard at one another for a minute. Lots of "ifs" and "buts" needed filling in, but it appeared to be part of the answer we were looking for.

"Rick," Sue said. "Could Josh Holston have taken the theme of FTNF to heart to the extent that he would commit such a heinous act?"

"Racist beliefs, disorder through violence and terrorism. Yes," I said. "He had to. Otherwise none of this makes sense."

Sue looked back at the book and then at me again. Her eyes misted over, she took a deep breath, her shoulders rose as her lungs filled. Then they fell with the release of air as she took it all in. I leaned to her and took her hand. She was wearing a blue sapphire ring, a Lindy Star. It reflected her personality—a shining star in the dark. Her hand was warm. I remembered warm hands from another time.

I shook my head clear of those thoughts, releasing her hand too quickly. She looked up to me.

My ringing telephone brought us back to life and I excused myself to the house. The phone was on the kitchen counter next to my power juicer. I picked up the cordless hand set and brought it back to the porch where Sue was drying her eyes on the sleeve of her sweater.

"Hello," I said.

"Rick? This is Jim Harris."

"Hello, Chief. Is there something wrong?"

"Yes and no," he said. "First, there won't be a trial with regards to Evermore and Crenshaw."

"Is that the 'yes' or 'no' part of 'is something wrong?'"

"I'll let you be the judge of that," he said. "Second, Josh Holston is dead."

I took the phone from my face and looked at it as if I needed to see Jim Harris to confirm what he'd told me. He hadn't really said that, had he? Sue was staring at me. I gave her a blank look.

"Rick?" Jim said. "You there?"

"Yah, chief," I said. "I'm here, but I can't believe what you just said. What happened?"

"It was a damned freak accident," Jim said. "The jailers at Denver County were moving Holston from a cell in the minimum security dormitory to a second floor cell in the maximum security building when Holston slipped going up the steps. He fell backwards and his foot caught in between the metal frame of the stairs. I was told that the angle of the fall caused him to flip over the side of the stairs. His foot loosened from the frame and he fell 15 feet to the floor, landing on his head. The fall broke his neck. He died on the spot."

Sue saw my expression. "What's wrong?"

I looked at her. "Josh Holston is dead."

"Oh, my God . . ." She was up and by my side very quickly. "How did it happen?"

I looked at her, and after a moment, pressing the fingers of my left hand to my forehead, I said, more to the floor than to her, "He was hit by karma and a two-by-four pine board."

EIGHTEEN

Early next morning I went to Jim Harris's office. Sue had left my place last night shortly after I'd told her what Jim had told me. She was not as saddened as I thought she would be. In fact, her demeanor was strangely happy, with a touch of satisfaction mixed in.

The outside air had that feel of warmer days ahead as it often does in the mountains. The sun was already bright and intense at 7:30 a.m. though the trees hid a cooler affect in their shade. One could already tell Estes Valley would receive Mom Nature's special gift of eighty degrees or better on this day. Summer had more or less officially begun. Life would get back to normal again. It had to. And the policing of Estes Park would take on new dimensions with tourist season upon us. The police force would take a dozen or so extra officers on part-time duty to cover all areas of community needs, which would last pretty much through the middle of August.

When I'd started working as one of those part-timers a few years ago, I found it not so different from teaching. I dealt with a lot of kids who needed discipline, both in the classroom and on the streets. Arrests would go up as traffic increased and vehicles and people filled Elkhorn Avenue from east to west. Jim would be especially busy for the summer. But with Holston's death, Jim's caseload had suddenly become much lighter.

"Morning, Jim," I said.

He looked up from his desk. "Oh, morning, Rick. It hasn't been a week since the shooting and the night you and Sue Richy spent tapping into those computers and cell phones, but it seems like a lifetime ago, doesn't it?"

"Yah," I agreed.

"Well, as I told you last night, this case is thankfully closed. Josh's funeral is this Saturday at the Methodist Church in Allenspark, where the Holston family originates and most are buried. Personally, I'm relieved it isn't here. It's too soon. Too heavy with grief and anger for us to one day bury the dead and the next day bury their killer."

I looked at Jim, sighed and nodded. "What about Josh's death?"

"An autopsy and coroner's inquest will be held," said Jim. "That'll determine both the cause of Holston's death and if the death was accidental and officially stop this machine they call justice . . . case closed.

"But what can I help you with, Rick? Whether you believe it or not, you did the department a great service with your help. If there's anything . . ."

"There is," I said. "We may never know what motivated Josh to kill those two kids. And maybe it doesn't matter now that he's dead. But because he *is* dead and he died without telling us anything, I personally need to come to some kind of an end for me."

"What? Are you somehow taking the blame for what happened?"

"If I had intervened," I said, "two good kids would be alive today. So, yes, I do take the blame. My job was to pay attention to the Josh Holstons of this world, Chief!"

"To do what, Rick?"

"My job is to keep kids grounded in where their lives are taking them. If they're going out of control, I rein them in. That is what I do. But I didn't do that with Josh. I ignored his needs and looked the other way and denied the possibilities when all along I knew there was an undercurrent of violence curdling in that boy's bloodstream. I lacked the courage to follow through and do my goddamned job, Jim."

"Whoa, whoa there big guy," he said, putting his hands up. "You're just one man and you're a good man. This affair had no bookmark on it that automatically linked to you. There is neither an 'all-knowing, all-seeing' clause written into your contract nor is that a part of your job description. Goddamn it anyway, Burns! This was not your fault."

With every phrase Jim's voice had gathered strength until I cringed away from him a bit. He was good!

"This is why you're chief, Chief, "I said. "You almost had me convinced. Now, may I ask a favor?"

"Sure! Ask for the goddamned moon for all I care."

I waited for him to cool a bit. Then I went on. "Do you have computer access to names of known criminals where I can run a search?"

Jim had come back down. "Certainly I do. Our base has over ten thousand names of small to big time crooks. If they ever had their fingerprints taken, their names are on file. Do you have a name?"

"Yah, I have a couple of names," I said.

"Do these names have anything to do with Holston?"

"They might."

"And if I were give you access to information in the computer, what would your intentions be toward these people if you would happen to find their names?"

"I really have no intentions, Jim, if I catch your drift," I said. "I would be interested in connections."

"And in order to connect, how would you propose to act?"

"Jesus, Jim!" I said. "I don't know what the hell my intentions would be or how I'd act on the information! Why the hell would it matter . . . Jesus!"

"Relax, Rick." Jim looked closely at me. "I'm curious. I wouldn't want you doing anything drastic or illegal."

"Who, me?" I said. "Look, the other night in your station, I found that there might be some way to explain Holston's actions. We never had the opportunity to explore the possibility. I realize it does nobody any good now. But because Holston is dead doesn't mean his rationale isn't still very much alive. I want to know for myself, to find out where I screwed up with this kid and maybe prevent it from happening again."

"Okay," Jim said. "I needed to know where you were coming from on this. I'm not supposed to let just anybody use this information, but I see your point and I have sympathy for you and I owe you one. If you would explain a little more about how you came on to this information, enlighten a friend a little, and I may be more comfortable with this."

I told Jim about the hate-groups book and the probable FTNF connection. Jim was not surprised by the racist theory, and saw a possible connection. He became interested in the possibility of co-conspirators, in the sense of influence, though not actual physical presence. Nothing that would affect the case as it was now, nothing the law would be interested in, as it concerned the murders. In the eyes of the law, this case was closed.

"Give me the names," he said, "and let's see where it takes us. Then we'll talk about where it'll take you. I'm a little concerned."

"Fine." I met Jim's eyes and held the stare until he looked away.

Jim turned to his computer. With a few clicks, he put us into the system which was protected by software and coded entries to prevent people like me from overstepping our bounds, I suppose. I stood behind him and watched.

Once in, he typed the name, "Jones, Manson (Mac)." The search fired up and within seconds we had the answer.

Jones had been arrested five years ago for burning a black church in Mississippi and was presently serving time at Parchman Farm, which is a nice name for the Mississippi State Penitentiary.

Jim looked at me, "Well, there's one of the two. Let's have the other name Rick."

I handed him "Terrence (Terry) Sims" and, again, seconds after Jim entered the name, the results were there on the screen. Sims had repeated arrests and had served time for assault and battery, for terrorizing and domestic assault. He'd served some time three years ago in a local jail in Greenwood, Mississippi. His last known address was Garden City, Kansas.

"Terrence must have run out of favor with the fine people of Greenwood," I said.

"Or something," said Jim. "But either way, there you have it. If the organization is still in force there are other leaders or, most likely, the organization has died a natural death. Let's hope the latter is true."

"Right," I said. "Whatever connection these two had with Holston was probably in Holston's mind. There's nothing that could link one with the other, at least not in a court of law."

I straightened, and stepped away from his desk.

"Well, thanks a million, Jim," I went on. "Good of you to let me see this. I'm sure you're right about the connection, or rather the lack of connection between Holston and this bunch."

Jim nodded. "You and I will officially end this here, okay? The summer is beginning and I'll be calling on you to help the department over the Fourth. Rumor has it that you asked for an extension on signing a contract for next year. You thinking of leaving us?"

I looked deadpan at him. He caught on.

"Well, I hope you change your mind," he said. "You're one of the good ones. But now I have to be excused. I have chaos control to deal with from now till September." He walked to the door, holding it open for me.

"Bye, chief," I said. "Maybe I'll apply for a full-time job with your department."

"I'd take you in a Mercury minute, but the kids need you in that school," he said. And the door closed.

I was on the street, a street that had warmed up considerably, with morning traffic already thick coming up from Loveland way.

Before heading for home, I drove to the cemetery. I parked on the narrow strip of blacktop lane that ran by the headstone of the Evermore family. I got out and walked over to the site. A small hill of dirt covered Bob's casket. I said a short prayer to no one in particular. Then I walked the thirty yards or so to the Crenshaw family plot, stood at Amy's final resting place and said the same prayer. But it really wasn't a prayer as much as it was a promise, a promise to find out why, for their sakes. That was my vow. It was as much to my guilt and my own conscience as it was to them. I would find out why and I would make sure it didn't happen again.

I looked out past the graves beyond the city and to the

distant Rockies and promised the mountains that this would not happen again.

NINETEEN

I rang up Shields' Insurance on my slider cell. Steve answered.
"Hi, Steve," I said.
"Hey, buddy," he said. "I've been wondering about you. What's up?"
"It's about 8:30 a.m. in my world and I haven't had breakfast. If you aren't busy, want to meet at Starbucks on the river? My treat."
"Did you say you're treating? It's a blessed miracle!"
"Smart ass," I said. "See you there in ten minutes."
"I'm holding you to that."
The shaded river walk with the Big Thompson running alongside is a nice respite from reality. Steve and I found a table, where we sat to catch up with one another. Steve picked a Columbia Narino Supreme and I an Arabian Mocha Sanani, both Grande, with lemon bars and blueberry muffins on the side. Tourists walked along the way, enjoying the day and the sights. Families with young children stopped by the river's edge, peered over the water wall and studied the swift flowing river for evidence of trout. It was a relaxing setting and seemed a million miles away from hate and violence and death.
After the first sip of brew, I said to Steve, "How did it go with the Evermores and the insurance?"
"Oh, shit. That is the last thing an insurance man wants to bring to a house of grief. But I had to. Larry and Cecilia are wonderful people. Bob was their only child. The policy had a twenty thousand dollar death benefit attached. Standard in that type of policy. It rarely ever pays out. The intent of the policy is to generate funds for college when the recipient becomes eighteen."

Here he paused a minute to collect his thoughts. I waited, knowing he'd get it out in his own time.

"When they saw me at the door, they had no clue why I was there other than as a friend to offer condolences. Which I was of course there to do, also. But they had to know of the business side of the policy, and when I told them that a check would be arriving in a few weeks for the amount, I felt terrible. This was not the good news it should have been had Bob been alive and just beginning his college career. Rick, they stared at me and I saw the utter look of hopelessness in their eyes. They took the policy envelope I offered to them and dropped it to the ground as if the value meant nothing, less than nothing. And I felt the same way. I just turned and left the house. Hardest damn thing I ever had to do."

"'The Monkey's Paw,'" I said, mostly to myself.

"What?"

"Oh, nothing . . . 'The Monkey's Paw' is a short story."

"Well, what the hell does that have to do with this?" Steve sounded a little pissed.

"Sorry," I said. "'The Monkeys Paw' shows how fate can throw a wrench into our otherwise contented lives."

"Enlighten me," he said.

"As the story goes, three wishes are granted to a family. They're warned that their third wish will be for death. The family ignores the warning. They wish for money. The money comes to them but at a terrible price. It comes to them as a benefit resulting from the tragic death of their only son, and the news of that death and said benefit was handed to them by an agent much like you, Steve."

"Jesus. You scare me sometimes."

"I scare myself," I said.

"So, you started this. Finish it. What were the other two wishes?"

"The second wish was for their son to return to them alive," I said.

"What's so bad about that?"

"It's okay," I said with a shrug. "Let's talk about something else."

"No, you dumb shit," he said.

I sighed. "Remember how Bob Evermore died?"

"Holston shot his head off from behind, the sonofabitch. I'm glad he's dead."

"In the story," I continued, "the son died as a result of being pulled into the machinery at a factory where he worked. His body was disfigured beyond recognition."

Steve was quiet and I was sorry I'd started this. He looked at me, waiting, as I hesitated.

"Well, the wish for their son to return to life came true," I said, "but he came back to life in the form in which he'd died... mutilated beyond recognition. When this realization came to the family, and as the son was at the front door in the middle of the night, knocking to be let in, the third wish was made and it was for death, their son's death. When the door was finally opened there was nothing there, nothing to be seen. The end." I was done now and wished I hadn't said a thing.

"Sheesh, Rick. You teach this to kids?"

"There's a lesson to be learned from fiction," I said.

"I get it. But, sheesh."

My coffee needed refreshing. I got up to do that while Steve sat, looking out over the view. Inside the store, while waiting for a refill, I looked around for familiar faces. Dan Green and his wife, Sidney, were sitting at a corner table, sharing a muffin with what looked like a couple of black teas. Dan noticed me and waved. Sidney turned and waved. I smiled and nodded back at them. All other faces were strange to me.

Back outside, Steve and I sat quietly for a few minutes, letting in the sights and sounds of the busy morning: senior citizens leisurely promenading along the walk, kids playing and chasing about in front of their parents, young mothers pushing baby strollers and the rich walking their poodles and setters, leashed, an extension of the owners' arms.

"Steve?" I said.

"Yah?"

"I have to find out why Holston did this."

He looked at me as though I were mad.

"And just why the hell does it matter?" he asked.

"It matters to me." I stared into my coffee cup. "It matters to me."

He saw that, for whatever reason, I was serious.

"How do you propose to do that, my friend?" he asked. "Holston is certainly not going to tell you. Without his input, you're kind of screwed, aren't you?"

"In a way, I think he left a clue for me." Here I explained my theory of FTNF while Steve listened quietly. Then I resumed, "And whether or not it matters to any one else, there are more kids like Josh Holston who are out there and are prime targets for this kind of racial hatred, and if I can stop what it is that draws others like Holston into the same mindset he was in, to do what he did, then I just have to do it."

Steve said, "Are you taking on the guilt for what happened at Dempsey's? It wasn't your fault. You're not obligated to go out and save all the poor dispossessed Josh Holstons of the world."

"Maybe not, but maybe I can make a small mark. Anyway, I'm going to take off for a week or two to find out some answers. It'll require me to do a little driving."

"Okay, okay, my friend. I understand," said Steve, uncertainty in his voice. "Will you at least keep in touch?"

"Sure. I'll be all right."

At this Steve's cell phone rang and he answered. "Yep. I'll be at my office at . . ." He looked at his watch. "At ten-thirty. Right . . . see you there." He hung up, returning the phone to his pocket. He took a final sip of his drink, saying, "Gotta make a living."

He got up from the table, started turning away. Turning and walking backwards, he said, "Remember to call me when you get to whatever conclusion you get to."

"I love you too, Mr. Shields!" I replied. Then Steve was gone.

I'd said that last a little too loudly. An elderly couple sitting at the table next to us special-delivered to me a four-eyed stare that would have wilted a smaller man.

I stood. "Lovers spat," I whispered to them. I leaned over to the man and kissed him on his bald head.

"Oh, my Lord," I heard the old lady say as I walked casually away, my right forearm lifted up and out, my right wrist ninety-degree angled.

TWENTY

Years ago I bought a bright yellow American Tourister Gear duffle bag, large enough to haul around a week's worth of clothes and sundries. The bag fit comfortably in the trunk of the Miata with some room to spare, though Miatas are not known for spacious trunk appeal. I never figured why the damned car battery was located in the trunk and not up front with the engine, till I looked under the hood. "The well was full" there, as they say. I pulled the duffle from the hall closet, threw it on the bed and began to think of my intentions.

I wasn't really clear on intentions, to be honest. I knew I wanted to find out more about FTNF. I needed to understand how Josh had been influenced by the organization. In order to do that, I needed to talk to people. I had two in mind: Mac Jones and Terry Sims. Jones was in prison and Sims was in Garden City. So I was going to Kansas and Mississippi. What I was going to say or do, I had not a clue. But I knew that whatever it was I had to do would demand a sort of courage on my part, to confront the kind of hatred these two men apparently spewed. Plus, it was the right thing to do, for the sake of kids like Josh Holston.

With little to no plan and little courage, I packed the bag with my shaving kit, a pair of Lee jeans, khaki shorts, five pairs of underwear, three pairs of socks, one long-sleeved white-with-blue-stripes Van Heusen shirt, a Minnesota Twins baseball cap and three logo tee-shirts: Salty Dog Café of Hilton Head Island, Denver Broncos and "I Got Half-Sauced" at Half Sauced BBQ, Lake of the Ozarks where, by the way, their beans and pulled pork are the best. My traveling clothes included a CU Buffs gold and black tee, Lands' End denims and New

Balance trainers. There was enough room for my Dell laptop tucked between the layers of clothes and I threw in a pair of swim trunks just because there was room. If the need arose, I'd find a washer/dryer somewhere.

I picked up Rand McNally to bring along for quick referral, checked the wallet for cash, credit and debit cards, driver's license and medical card. Proof of insurance for the Miata was in the glove compartment (I never kept gloves in that compartment). All my documents were in order. I was covered for everything except Armageddon.

I double-checked the back door. It was still locked from the twenty minutes ago when I'd first checked it. Gas and water were shut off, leaving just the front door to secure and I'd be out of here.

As I opened the door there stood Sue Richy, arm poised to knock. Shit.

"Where are you going?" she asked.

"Uh, hi to you, too, Sue," I said. "I'm . . . uh, going to town to pick up a few grocery items."

"Oh," she said. "And do you always carry your duffle bag with you when you go, uh, shopping, as you so cleverly say?"

"Yes," I lied, and walked past her to my car. I clicked open the trunk with my remote and, throwing the bag in, closed it up again.

"What are you up to, Sue, and what brings you out here this fine afternoon?" I asked. The best defense is a good offense.

Sue was wearing a tan cotton men's button-down collared shirt, knotted at the front, showing the slightest hint of tanned skin, and sleeves rolled up to the elbows, Eddie Bauer jeans and flip flops. Her toenails were painted a light red, which matched her nails. Her hair was swept back from her face and kept in place with a headband. She looked as though she was ready either to clean house or take a long ride.

Uh, oh.

"I spoke with Steve Shields an hour ago," she said, glaring at me.

And with that she turned and walked down the three steps of the porch, to the yard and to her VW. She opened the passenger side door. From her car she pulled a black Nike duffle bag. She turned from the car, remotely locked its doors with a backward flick of her wrist while walking determinedly to the Miata.

She said, "Open the trunk, please."

I was trapped. I pushed the button, releasing the lock.

Sue threw her bag in next to mine, closed the lid, and walked to the passenger side of the Miata. She asked, "Is this door unlocked?"

"Yes," I said. My jig was up.

"Thank you," she said. She pulled open the door and in she went, butt first, of course. It is a Miata, after all.

I was still on the porch as this motion picture developed in front of me. Yes, my jig was definitely up. I nearly forgot to lock the front door. But I pulled myself together, locked the door and went to the Miata, getting in behind the wheel. I had put the top up earlier as it looked like the daily rain shower was inevitable. A Miata is small enough with the top down but with the top up, it was close inside. Once in, I looked over to Sue.

She looked back and said, "Your jig is up."

This woman was spooky-smart.

"Rick, I know you've taken on some kind of guilt for what happened," she went on. "I think I understand some of what you feel. I want to help you, if I can. You don't have the monopoly on guilt here. Two can share in that particular emotion. I'm sticking with you till you get through whatever it is you have to get through. Perhaps it'll help me, too."

She took the road map from me and asked, "So . . . where are we going?"

TWENTY-ONE

I like to think I'm an intelligent man who knows when to hold 'em and when to fold 'em. I'd just got beat by an inside straight. I folded, for the time being.

"Garden City, Kansas," I said.

Sue opened the map to the United States overview of interstate roadways and said, "Take 36 south to Boulder, to the Denver-Boulder Turnpike, to Interstate 70, east."

She closed the map and leaned her head back, stretching those hurdler's legs as far as the car allowed, and gazed out the passenger side window.

Well, hell, I knew where I was going and how. I didn't need a woman to tell me. But maybe now wasn't the time to bring that up. She must have needed the power of map control. I sensed that the conversation ball was in my court, yet there was no time restraint on putting it to use until I was ready.

I started the car, pulled away from my house and drove toward Estes Park. The gas tank was full. We were good for three hundred miles, maybe even more, as it was downhill to Boulder. It was also 2:00 in the afternoon. I'd decided earlier to drive to Garden City in one stretch. It was a four hundred mile drive, but now I needed to consider another player in this scenario, and a woman at that. But I figured Sue had come into this without questioning my personal travel plans. In my mind, I would stop when I wished to stop, eat where I wished to eat and sleep when and where I wished to do so. Sue would just have to go along with it. My car, my call. But red flags were up and waving all around. She should not be here.

I had kept the top up even though it was warm out. I put the air on and this kept the Miata quite comfortable. I used the air on long hot trips to keep from sunburning, because that mountain sun with the thin atmosphere does its damage to exposed skin. When I do keep the top down on long rides, I generally wear my cap and a long-sleeved shirt with sunscreen applied to lips, nose, and high cheeks.

We were well on to 36 past Lake Estes and the mountain curves took my attention, but I heard Sue's breathing soften and knew she was asleep. I took a quick look at her. Like her breathing, her skin was smooth. Her neck was turned slightly away from me and I noticed a blue vein running up to her hair line behind her left ear. She had a scent I hadn't been aware of till now, musky but not overwhelming. Her hair drawn back from her face was touchable, and I nearly reached over to move a strand that had fallen out of place and was lying across her left cheek.

That would be a stupid thing to do, I thought. Shit. Shit. Shit!

I didn't need this. Sue Richy was not supposed to be a part of my plans. She would only be in the way and slow down progress in searching for the answers I knew I could find on my own. Delayed anger syndrome was my response to Sue's blatant intrusion into my life.

Goddamn it any way, now I was really annoyed. I thought of stopping the car right there and telling her to amscray. I should get her smart little black Nike bag out of my car, throw it out into the ditch and tell her, "Good luck!" and leave her there.

I was huffing and puffing when Sue woke with a start and turned to me, those blue eyes half opened, dreamy, trusting. Shit. Double Shit!

"Hi," I said, an effing coward to the end.

"Hi." She turned her whole body toward me and I could tell she was now looking for dialogue. So, I aimed to please.

"We're just coming through Denver and we're on I-70 directly south of Denver International," I said. "If all goes well, we should be in Garden City somewhere around ten o'clock tonight."

"I guess I acted without thinking," she said. "I'm sorry. But when Steve told me about your plan, I felt cheated. I've been with you through this whole nasty business these past two weeks and I thought leaving me out at this point wasn't fair. I'm the kind of girl who takes the bull by the horns."

"Don't I know it." I gripped the steering wheel hard. "You blindsided me back there in Estes Park. What I do is my business. You were not invited. It took guts and a certain amount of disdain for you to hitch a ride on this wagon for whatever purpose I have. I'm not amused by you in the least. I would rather you had found other ways and means to handle your personal guilt. Instead here you are, compounding my troubles. Jesus, Sue."

She replied, "I wouldn't blame you if you sent me back home from the nearest bus station."

"And don't think I haven't thought about that!" I said, and glanced at her. "The feeling temporarily passed."

Sue turned back to face the front. "Thanks. How fast does this little thing go?"

"It's a Mazda Speed MX-5, not a 'little thing' thanks very much." Now she was irritating. "We're going seventy-five mph and can go 135 if the need arises."

"Sorry again," she said. "MX-5, Mr. Sensitive." She turned and poked me in the ribs.

"Don't do that!"

"Don't do what? You mean this?" She poked me again.

"Yes, that!" I laughed at her. She was good.

"Okay." She looked to the front again. "I have been a bad girl, Mr. Burns. I will not poke you in the ribs again." She turned and did it again. "Excuse me, please." She giggled.

We stopped at a McDonalds along the interstate. Miatas forego the need to order at windows. There is just not enough room to eat two meals comfortably inside a traveling MX-5, so we parked and went in.

We first took the bathroom detour and then ordered. I had a burger, fries and small drink (love that dollar menu). Sue ordered an oriental salad and bottled water, insisting on paying her own way. I didn't argue. Hell, she made almost as much money as I.

I noticed that Sue gathered attention from the male eyes as we walked to a table by the window.

She was attractive. I didn't question that. But that was not what this was about. Besides, old hurts rose to the surface and I dismissed any wayward thoughts. Our table looked out at traffic on I-70, a mixture of cars and trucks passing along either way toward Kansas or Denver.

My sandwich was palatable and the fries were addicting. Sue picked at her salad, avoiding the croutons and the extra dressing pack. She looked at me with a critical eye when I reached for the salt. I noted that, withdrew my hand and picked up a squeeze-pack of ketchup instead.

I noticed that she physically separated her vegetables, and went for the lettuce first. Then she ate the mandarin orange slices, but saved the spinach leaves for last. I could have criticized, but didn't quite know how to argue the point.

"What's in Garden City, Kansas?" She took a sip of water from the bottle, and then screwed on the plastic cap.

"The two names associated with FTNF, Mac Jones and Terry Sims? Well, Jones is vacationing at Parchman Farm in Mississippi, which is the state prison. Armed robbery conviction. Sims has served time for various hate crimes convictions but is out and has moved to Garden City where it seems he has family. And you know, 'Family is the one place where, when you have to go there, they have to take you in.' I want to talk to both of them. Looks like Sims is the natural first choice, at least in the geographical sense."

"What do you want from them?" she asked.

"I want to know what motivates men like that to do what it is they seem to have to do. Understanding that may clue me in on why Josh Holston did what he did. Understanding that may help stop the next killing. There has to be a deterrent to this hatefulness. I want to harness it and bring it back home and bury it."

"And what if you fail?"

"I can't fail."

"Then we won't," she said matter-of-factly.

Oh, it was "we" now, was it? She had a little too much spirit for her own good.

When we got back to the car, I suggested taking the top down. The sun was falling away and would be behind us, and temps were summer-warm. I enjoyed driving with the top down in the early twilight into evening. The rush of air around the car was like taking in pure oxygen, refreshing and exhilarating with the open sky above.

Sue said she had no problem with that. The top was down in twenty seconds and I impressed her with the Miata's on-ramp speed, eighty mph came quite quickly as we blended back into the lightened west-east traffic on the interstate.

TWENTY-TWO

The steady drone of the engine soon put Sue back to sleep. Her hair tossed about her face as the wind swept around to our backs. Maybe this will work out. Maybe I was a little harsh on Sue. Time would tell.

We crossed into Kansas. I enjoyed shifting back and forth from fifth gear to sixth and back again to pass vehicles with the Miata's turbo-enhancement. It varied the tedium of travel. At the Goodland exit I stopped at a BP station for gas. Sue woke up as I drove the off-ramp, into the station and up to a pump. I got out and swiped my credit card. High octane quenched the little engine's thirst. I asked Sue if she needed anything.

"No, thanks," she said. "I'll just stretch a bit. I wish my VW was a convertible. The air feels so good. How much farther?" She was out of the car, yawning, with her arms angling upward, reaching for the stars. Then she leaned over the frame of the car, reached behind the seat where she had earlier stuffed Mr. Rand McNally.

I said, "It's about three hours nonstop from here. We'll get off I-70 at U.S. 83 in about forty minutes. It's all two-way at that point. That should get us there at ten, give or take."

"Okay," she said without concern, and put the atlas back. "I guess I'll take a quick look at my face before we head out." And off she went.

There was nothing wrong with that face.

We pulled in to a Best Western on the north end of Garden City at 10:00. I stopped the car at the front entrance. Sue stayed in the car while I got checked for rooms. The manager at the front desk, Roger, by his name tag, told me he had plenty of rooms. I asked for two rooms, nonsmoking, one bed, two nights, one person in each room.

Roger said, "Yes sir." He told me that rooms 224 and 226 would be quite comfortable, to drive around to the back and enter the center door. He gave me two card keys.

I thanked him.

Roger said, "Good night, sir."

Sir . . . I liked that.

Back at the Miata I asked Sue, "Do you want the key to door number 224 or door number 226?"

"Isn't there a third door?"

"Yes there is," I said. "The out-of-doors"

She started to laugh and said, "I'll take the room closest to the exit."

I threw her a card and she caught it one-handed. I was impressed.

I drove to a spot in the back and we got out of the car. I put the top up, locked the doors and opened the trunk. Sue picked up her Nike duffle and I my yellow duffle, shut the trunk and, using the card key to open the locked back entrance, we made our way up a flight of stairs and found the rooms.

At her door, Sue said, "Give me a copy of the billing so I can pay my share. I insist." I gave her the copy and she folded it. "Thanks," she said, sticking it in a side zippered pouch of her bag.

"Good night," I said. "I'll see you around eight for breakfast and we'll talk about plans."

"Okay. G'night."

I started to walk away.

"Rick?" The hallway stretched behind her in green and red tartan patterns. "Thanks for taking me along."

"As if I had a choice?"

She smiled and disappeared into 224.

I slid my card in the lock and opened the door to a comfortable room. Under the window was the usual motel air condition blower which I could set to "freeze" and I did. There was a queen bed, reading light above the headboard, bed stand with electric clock and telephone, a work desk for laptop, television cabinet with TV and luggage table, bath with shower and hair blower and thick towels. Everything a weary traveler could possibly want.

I plugged in my cell phone to recharge and found a telephone book. I opened it, finding three Sims in the Garden City area: Sarah, Eugene and Terry. That seemed almost too easy. Too easy generally turns into something else.

There had to be a twist here that I wasn't aware of but would soon find out, I'd bet. I decided to wait till tomorrow, and I hit the bed sheets, more tired than I'd realized. No more mind-wandering tonight. There was work to do and courage to muster.

TWENTY-THREE

Sue and I met in the breakfast area just off the main lobby. There were a few other travelers at the buffet of rolls, fruits, cereals and coffee dispensers. The morning news was broadcasting on a large screen TV sitting in one corner of the room. *USA Today* newspapers were strewn about on tables where other guests had already come and gone. Roger was still at the lobby desk, tending to checkouts, exhorting have-a-nice-days and come-see-us-agains.

Sue and I sat. I had a coffee and glazed donut while she had water and an orange. I looked at her as she peeled the orange, placing the segments on a plastic plate. She moved the segments into a circle and proceeded to single out one at a time. She looked up at me and, seeing that I was watching her, gave me a more-superior-than-thou gaze and continued to eat. I made a mental note of that.

"I have a phone number for a Terry Sims. I found it in the phone book last night," I said after we'd finished with breakfast. "Let's go out to the car where we'll have some privacy. I'll call the number and see where it takes us. Okay?"

"So it begins, Mr. Burns." She looked at me for reassurance.

I didn't have a lot to give.

Out in the car, I opened my phone and punched in the number. Two rings and an automated voice told me the number had been disconnected.

"I figured it was too easy," I said.

"What next?"

"Ask around, I suppose. It works on TV."

We drove to a truck stop close to the motel. As we walked to the building, I checked out the Kansas landscape. It was broad and flat, extending in all directions. Wheat and cattle country. Dodge City lay to the east on US 50; the new Old West. I looked toward the rising sun. The day would be a warm one.

There was a dining area inside the truck stop. We went in and sat at a table. I wanted information, not food, but sacrifice is part of the deal. It was fairly busy, but a waitress spotted us and came to our table. Her name was Sheila, according to her nametag. We ordered . . . coffee for me and apple juice for Sue. As our waitress turned to go, I said, "Excuse me, Sheila."

She turned back to us. "Is there something else you'd like?"

"Nothing to eat, but I'm wondering if you could help us. We're looking for someone from Garden City and the phone number I called was disconnected. Do you know a family named Sims?"

"Oh, sure," she said. "Sarah Sims lives in my apartment complex. We went to high school together. Are you looking for her?"

"Actually," I said, "I'm looking for a Terry Sims."

Sheila's demeanor change was immediate.

"Is there something wrong?" I asked.

"Terry Sims is dead, thank you, God. Sorry, but if he's a friend of yours, you better be pickin' better friends."

"Oh, no, he's no friend," I hastened to say. "I just wanted to ask him a few questions."

Sheila sized me up. "Terry Sims came here a few years ago to stay with his Uncle Eugene and Aunt Bertha. That's Sarah's mom and dad. He was a bad person and a racist pig. He caused nothing but trouble for his relatives. But they had to take him in you know, family and all."

At this I looked at Sue, lifting my eyebrows in an "I told you so" fashion.

"He was family and Uncle Eugene felt some obligation toward him. Least that's what Sarah told me."

"Where could I find Terry and Eugene?" I asked.

"They're both over at Valley View Cemetery. Eugene works there. He cuts grass and takes care of flowers on graves and such. And Terry's buried there. 'Scuse me, I got an order come up."

Well, that changed things a little. We drank our drinks. I left a five dollar tip for a two dollar tab. Sue paid the bill. She was a stickler.

Valley View Cemetery was located on the north side of town. We found it easily and drove in. Cemeteries are small towns in themselves, with streets and neighborhoods of graves and always an open plot somewhere. I drove to the northwest side of the cemetery and found a maintenance shed. A gray-haired man on a rider mower was going toward the shed from a side lane. I parked the car and Sue and I got out, waited for the man to dismount from the mower. He saw us and turned the mower off.

"Howdy, friend," he shouted louder than was necessary. The roar of the mower engine was still probably fresh in his ears. "Can I help ya?"

"Are you Eugene Sims?" I asked.

"Well, today is your lucky day young fella. I am Eugene Sims who mows grass and God willin' tomorrow will find me still Eugene Sims and still mowin' grass." He laughed a hearty belly laugh and we couldn't help but laugh along.

"Mr. Sims," I said. "My name is Rick Burns and this is Sue Richy. We've come from Colorado."

"Colorado, eh," he said. "That's one beautiful state ya got there, and that's one beautiful gal by yer side too." He chortled.

"Yes, isn't she though?" We both looked at Sue, appraising her in a dignified way.

Sue blushed.

"Mr. Sims," I went on. "We were wondering about your nephew Terry."

And with that, all humor left the old guy and he eyed us with suspicion. "And just what about my nephew were ya wonderin'?"

I looked at Sue and she whispered, "The truth will set you free."

I explained to Sims what had brought us to this place. He simply nodded as the story unfolded. When I'd finished, he said, "I heard about those killin's on the television. I'm rightful sorry. Pardon me, but when I heard Terry's name I hoped his friends weren't coming to give me trouble. We've had enough of that since he came back. Me and Bertha, that's my wife, why we hold family to be the tie that binds us to our loved ones. When Terry called from Mississippi and asked to come live with us for a while, I knowed he had a troubled life and had done jail time. His daddy, my brother Lucas, died in a farm accident when Terry was a young kid. His Mama was a weak woman and Terry, like any kid, pushed her to the limits as he grew up. He quit school when he was sixteen years old and run in with a bad crowd."

"Was one of them Mac Jones?" I asked.

"Yes, the sumbitch," Sims said. "I never knowed Jones but I knowed what he led Terry into. Is that why yer here?"

I said, "Mr. Sims, we're here to try to find out why your nephew became a part of an organization called FTNF, which we believe influenced the young boy in Colorado to do what he did."

Sims leaned heavily against the mower. "I heard Terry talk about that FTNF crap. He was full of hate, Mr. Burns. But he was taken to be that way. Like I says, he growed up without a daddy and he had no real direction from his mama. We always lived out here in the middle of nowhere and had little contact with him. We ain't rich people. Hell, we ain't even poor people. We ain't that high up. But Terry, he took to bad ways and he got into trouble and like I says, he ended up comin' out here when his buddy, that Jones fella, ended up in prison. They tried to say Terry helped set fire to that church but couldn't prove it. He got off, but the town judged him guilty and made it so he had to git.

"We took him in 'cause I loved my brother and I thought livin' out here would do Terry some good. But he was just as mean-spirited as ever. He hated all black folks. These was his thoughts, not mine, you understand."

I nodded that I understood.

"He hated all the blacks and Jews and Catholics and he thought they was goin' to spoil the world by mixin' the races and weakenin' the religions, and then take it over and kill all the whites," he went on. "So Terry thought that the whites had to strike first and rid the world of all those type people. He said that the final task would never be done till the last of them was dead. Every task that he finished left more to be done, he thought. He said it would take a long time but if he got enough people who thought like him and his group, it would go quicker. But I thought he was all talk."

"Did you ever see any other people who Terry talked about joining his group?" I asked.

"Oh, sure," Sims said. "Some come to our house. I kicked 'em out and told 'em that if they was gonna talk that talk, they had to talk it somewhere else, not in my house!"

"What kind of people were they who came, Mr. Sims?" I asked.

"They were young kids. They all shared somethin' in common though. I seen it when I heard em talk. They all had a grudge of some kind, either with a parent or the police or somethin' else. They had no humor about em, ya know? Why, look at me. I got a sense of humor. None of those boys had a sense a humor. How can ya get along in life without ya got a sense a humor, now I ask?" Without waiting for my answer, Sims asked, "Was that boy in Estes Park like that?"

"Yes, he was, Mr. Sims," I said. "I heard that Terry died."

"Yah, he was in a car accident three weeks ago whilst driven' around with some of his buddies who come up from Mississippi. The car went into a ditch. He was in the back seat and was throwed out. The car landed on top of him as it rolled through the ditch." Here Sims stopped for a moment. "He was family and I can't help but feel sad for the boy. Of course he was forty two years old, not a boy any more. I'm seventy-two years old. I wished I coulda helped my nephew, but he was past help. I still feel bad."

"Where is he buried, Mr. Sims?" I asked.

"Oh, he ain't far from here. Let me show ya."

The old man deserved at least this regard for the help he gave us, and I could tell he truly felt saddened. Sue put her arm through mine and we followed Eugene just south of the maintenance shed to a small triangular plot of green grass. There were about fifteen stones in this area. He stepped up to a small marker that stated simply, TERENCE SIMS.

We stood for a long minute. I felt a little bad too, but not for Terry Sims. I felt bad for man's mortality, good or evil that we are. "It is the blight man was born for." The good die and the evil die. Perhaps there is a place they go to after all is said and done to live out eternity, in peace or in fire.

Mr. Sims turned to us, his humor returned. "Boy, ya know when I first saw you two come drive in with that little sports car, I thought you was tourists comin' to look at the Clutter graves."

I knew what Sims meant. What I didn't tell Sue was that I had been in Garden City before. I'd been in this very cemetery for a very different reason.

The Clutter family. Four innocents killed by two crazies back in the late 1950s. Capote wrote about it in his book, *In Cold Blood*. I taught that book several years ago. I remember seeing the original movie made back in the sixties. Ex-cons Perry Smith and his partner, Richard Hickock, drove to a lone farmhouse intent on robbing Herb Clutter of ten thousand dollars. Ended up, there was no money and the two would-be crooks became killers, shooting the entire family at their home: mother, father, a daughter and son. A second daughter, fortunately, was away at college at the time. The Clutters were buried together here in River View Cemetery. They rested less than fifty yards from where we stood.

"I'll show ya where theys restin,'" Eugene led us to the gravesite. Each child was resting on either side of the parents. All had the same date of death, 1959.

"November fifteenth, right, Mr. Sims?" I asked.

"That's right."

Sue said, "I saw the movie when I was younger. I'll never forget the man running from room to room and shooting those poor people. It was terrible what happened." She looked around. Mr. Sims was gone. She looked at me.

I said, "I acquired some trivia about the movie. Did you know that the house scenes of the movie were actually filmed in the original home?"

"You're kidding," she said.

"No, really."

"How creepy is that," she said. She still had hold of my arm while we lingered at the Clutter gravesite but let go as we walked back to the car. It was very quiet here. The only sounds were those of our footsteps on the gravel lane.

"We're basically done in Garden City," I said. "But I want you to take a little drive with me. I'd like you to see something."

"I'm rather a captive audience to you and your car, aren't I, Mr. Burns?" she said. "You like keeping me on my toes."

"And damned proud of it! Hop in."

We kept the top up and drove out to Highway 50 where I turned west, past the motel and out of Garden City proper. Seven miles later, I turned left at a sign that read, WELCOME TO HOLCOMB, FINNEY COUNTY, KANSAS.

"What's in this little town?" Sue asked.

"Lots of packing plants around this area," I told her. "Holcomb is just a small town with something I want to show you. Be patient."

I drove past a school and through town and continued toward the south end, crossing a set of railroad tracks, almost driving beyond the city limits when I turned on what appeared to be the last residential paved street, running west. At the end of about two blocks the street turned right, but what appeared to be a private tree-lined non-paved drive continued westerly. I kept going straight onto the dirt lane.

"What is this?" she asked. "You seem to know exactly where you're going."

"Do you remember anything more about the movie, *In Cold Blood*? You remember the inside of the house where the murders took place, but do you remember the outside of the house?"

Sue turned to me. "Where are we?"

"It's perfectly okay, Ms. Richy."

I continued the drive. It was only about an eighth of a mile. Trees lined the road on either side, obscuring the view. Ahead and to the right we could make out a house through the leaves, though not clearly. Then there it was, the Clutter home, just as it had been decades ago. Standing stark naked so to speak, wheat fields behind and to the sides. I drove onto the yard a bit and U-turned back to the lane but stopped just south of the structure. It looked as though time had frozen. There stood the simple frame home with a second story rising in the center, the main entrance at the left of center, another to the far right and another to the far left. In the center on the second level was a lone window. Nancy Clutter's room. She was seventeen years old when she died, the same age as Amy Crenshaw.

Sue shuddered. "Why are we here?"

"Look at this house, Sue. People who had no grudge against anybody in the world lived a normal life here. I still want to know, what motivates a seemingly sane person to do a seemingly crazy act? The two men who killed this family, it was said that if they'd acted singly, neither would have killed anyone in this house on that night, but the two of them together formed a third personality, and that personality killed the family. Maybe that's true, maybe it's bullshit.

"But that doesn't answer the question about Josh Holston does it? How could a seemingly sane young man commit a seemingly crazy act? I can't answer that question yet. He acted alone. Or did he? If he didn't, then what was the outside influence that created a killer personality? I have an idea from what Sims told us, but there's more to know. I need to know more about FTNF."

Sue was looking at the house. She said, "I remember now. The young girl had a horse, didn't she?"

"And that same horse was used in the making of the movie."

She looked at me, her voice a little shaky. "Let's go, Rick. This is too spooky. I don't like being here."

"I don't either. But it's like sacred ground in a morbid way. Someone lives here today, did you notice? It's a working farm. There are signs of life about the place."

At which point a large black shepherd came around the far corner of the house, looking our way. We drove back down the lane.

"Didn't the movie show the two killers driving down this very lane with these trees on either side?" asked Sue, her voice tight. "But wasn't it at night?"

"What if I said yes?"

"Just don't say another word. Get me out of here."

How could anyone live in that house? I thought as we drove away.

We went back to the motel. It was noon and checkout time. On the way up the stairs, Sue asked, "What happened to those two criminals, Smith and . . . what was the other man's name?"

"Hickock," I said.

"I remember the movie ending as one of the two was hanged."

"They both were hanged on the same night, April 14, 1965. They're even buried next to one another in Mt. Muncie cemetery, which is just a mile or so north of the Kansas State Penitentiary where they spent the last years of their own worthless lives before justice brought closure."

"How do you know that?"

"Good question. That movie and the book bothered me so much I felt compelled to go to Mt. Muncie Cemetery a couple of years back to make sure they were indeed dead and buried there. How appropriate that they lie side by side, their wicked bones mingling together under the ground, sinking deeper with each passing year as the rains wash down over them. It's only fair."

Sue looked at me. "How unfair for Bob and Amy to lie where they are."

TWENTY-FOUR

If Sue wasn't sure before, she knew with certainty now that I was on a serious mission. Yet instead of backing down from the task at hand, she appeared even more resolved to be a part of it. I did admire her for that.

Next morning we were refreshed and ready to go.

"We're going to Mississippi now," I said. "Obviously FTNF is alive and well, according to Mr. Sims. Terry is dead, Jones is in prison, but Sims told me his nephew's friends left after the funeral."

"Where are they now?"

"He said they went back to Mississippi, and I'm beginning to think it may get dangerous once I start speaking to live people."

"Then you'll need a wing-man," Sue said.

"Wing-woman," I said.

"Whatever."

We packed up and checked out. Roger had since been replaced by Desmond, who wished us a nice day with an invitation to come back again sometime.

We were in the car with the top down, looking at the map. I found myself looking instead at Sue. Her hair was down. She apparently didn't mind the wind effect with convertible travel. She had on khaki North Face hiking shorts and I couldn't help but notice how her legs seemed to go on forever. She wore a salmon-colored v-neck short-sleeved tee, with a soft exposure of cleavage. I missed half of what she was saying.

"Let's go to Wichita and south to Tulsa, then east to Fort. Smith, Ar-kansas," she suggested. "That'll take about ten hours, getting us there around 10:00 tonight."

"I agree," I said, catching up to her voice. "But I have to

caution you to watch your pronunciation of Arkansas."

"What do you mean, Mr. English teacher?"

"What I mean, Ms. Richy," I said in my best teacher voice, "is that it is okay, while in Kansas, to pronounce Arkansas as if it is Ar-Kansas, emphasizing the 'Kan,' but once you cross that state line into Oklahoma, you had better start pronouncing Arkansas with emphasis on the 'Ar,' keeping the 'as' silent, as in 'Arkans-a-w.' Or else our visit to that fine state may be cut short by angry natives."

"My, my Mr. Burns," Sue said in her best southern drawl. "Little ol' me wouldn't think of embarrassing little ol' you with any m-i-s-p-r-o-n-u-n-c-i-a-t-i-o-n, bless your heart." With that she poked my ribs hard and added, "May I drive?"

God help me!

TWENTY-FIVE

Fort Smith was a ten-hour drive. Sue was behind the wheel for half of that, and she was a good driver, though a little heavy on the pedal. You get to know your driving companion during an extended drive in a Miata. I knew that Sue Richy was an Olympic hurdler representing the University of Alabama. I asked her about life on campus in Tuscaloosa.

"I'm from Birmingham, born and raised, but I was always a 'Bama fan. Mom and Dad were 'Bama alums so it came naturally for me."

"Were you on full scholarship?"

"Yah. I ran a pretty good 400 hurdles and Title 9 allowed me equal opportunity for money. They offered, I accepted. Home was close, which my parents loved. It was a great five years. I came in running a 57.35 on the hurdles. By the time I was a senior I clocked a 54.22 season best. That qualified me for the Olympic tryouts, but I tripped on the last hurdle in the final heat and that kept me off the team. It was okay. I accepted that this stuff happens. There were a lot of people in this world worse off than I. I was blessed with the body to jump hurdles with some speed, but I was never promised this blessing would carry over to a world record or a trip to the Olympics. It did carry me to a school record at Alabama. I didn't ask even for that, but it happened and I was proud. My family was always there for me. I couldn't have asked for more. The Olympics would get along fine without me, I knew. And it did."

"You get your teaching degree at Alabama?" I asked.

"Yah. Track kept me out of school during the season. It took the extra year to finish up."

"Why Colorado?"

"I'd never been to the mountains in my life till I trained at Colorado Springs. It was love at first sight. I love running the hills and trails. I love the snow. It was a perfect fit for this gal. My parents moved to Florida two years ago. They come up to visit once a year and I go see them two or three times a year."

"How about a man?" I took a chance.

"A man?" she asked. "Rick, don't you know? I don't date men, you know what I mean? Number one, I'm a female athlete. Number two, I'm a female P.E. teacher and coach. You really didn't know that I tend toward women?"

She looked at me and nearly swerved off the road at my reaction.

"No!" she exclaimed. "I'm one hundred percent straight! But that's the damned stereotypical baggage that every female who happens to be an athlete drags along. Did you think I was telling you the truth?"

"Duh . . . no. I knew you were playing with me."

"You did not. You're a big fat liar, Rick Burns!"

"Okay, okay. I did believe you, but just for a second."

"And what did you think in that second?"

"It gets a little kinky. Can't tell you."

"Ouch . . ." Rib jab, hard, and a dirty look besides, but the car stayed on the road at least.

"But did you date?" I asked after she'd settled down and after my ribs stopped aching.

"I went with a guy at school for a couple of years. He was a high jumper from Georgia. He was a good person, but we were both driven to excel in our individual competitions and that took time away from any normal relationship. After school, he went his way and I mine. We parted friends and still are."

"So, you're not seeing anybody now?"

"No," she said. "Do you know of anybody who's available?"

"Let me think about that for a million years and I'll get back to you, okay?"

Sue said, "I know *you* don't date. Why's that?"

I looked straight ahead. Sara Reese was not going to be a topic of discussion. I was quiet. The fence was up but Sara was there beside me, mocking my love for her and the ring I had held

to her finger. It was still a large hurt. Sue was not Sara Reese.
Sue waited. Then she picked up on my reluctance.
"Sorry," she said.
"Not a big deal." I peered up at the sky. "Looks like rain."

TWENTY-SIX

The next few hours were quiet except for the traffic noise and a rainsquall at the Kansas, Oklahoma border. We saw the lightning from a distance and stopped at a rest area to both put the top up and take care of nature's business. The Miata rides close to the road and does just fine on windy days. The wind doesn't affect the body motion, and the rain has a special sound when it falls on the canvas top of a convertible, but more caution is needed on rain-washed roads. The squall turned into a steady drizzle till we came into the north side of Oklahoma City where it finally stopped.

We pulled into an Exxon station/KFC for a gas fill and supper. Sue liked the Original Recipe while I catered to Extra Crispy. Between the two of us we did justice to both with a side of "smashed" potatoes and slaw and coke and water to wash it all down.

I took the wheel, and after skirting the east side of Oklahoma City we got on I-40 with about a three-hour drive left to Fort Smith. We had been listening to the radio, but Sue said, "Enough is enough. If I hear one more country western song, I'm going to change religions." She reached forward and snapped off the radio. "What do you have in your CD player?"

"I have a six CD changer and I believe it's full," I told her. "I haven't listened to it for a couple of months and really don't remember what's in there, but feel free to check it out. My music appreciation is somewhat eclectic."

"No problem," said Sue. She pushed number one. The music began to play. "Who's this?"

"Amy Grant. It's her first Christmas Album."

"Christmas?"

"Christmas is good all year round. You have a problem with that?"

"Not this girl."

She pushed number two. The music began. Sue looked at me with a questioning look.

"'God Bless the Child,' Billie Holiday."

Sue went to push the next selection, but I stopped her.

"Before you go to the next CD, listen to track four on this one."

Sue advanced the CD to track four, and "Strange Fruit," in Billie Holiday's soulful voice poured from the speakers.

When the song ended, Sue looked at me. "This is terrible stuff, Rick. And so sad."

"Most of the whites who patronized the bar where she first sang this song, back in 1939 and 1940, walked out, but not all walked out. There were many whites who sympathized with the way things were. But Holiday was blackballed—excuse the pun—south of the Mason-Dixon Line for years. No radio played her songs. She had no live gigs, no interviews. Yet where she did sing, the public insisted her encore song of the night be 'Strange Fruit.' FTNF and other groups like them reflect the mentality of people who still glorify the text of the song."

"You're more than interested in just finding the reasons behind Josh Holston's actions, aren't you?" Sue said.

I turned to her. "I want to destroy FTNF, and I really don't care how but I wish you weren't here with me in this."

She turned off radio and said, "Okay, I understand. But I'm not going anywhere, Rick."

The ride was quiet until we came around the northern edge of Fort Smith. I pulled off I-40 at Highway 59 and found a Super 8, and parked by the front entrance.

Inside I found Mohan Patel anxious to serve my needs. I asked for two rooms, nonsmoking, one bed, one night, one person in each room. Mohan said, "Yes sir." Two rooms were available. We could take the very beautiful open staircase located directly behind us in the main lobby. Rooms 212 and 214 were at the top of the steps to our left. The breakfast bar would be ready at 5 a.m. I could park right out front.

I gave Sue the billing for her records. We carried our bags upstairs and split up at our rooms, Sue taking 212 as it was closer to the stairs. When she asked what time in the morning I said, "How about 5:00?"

She said, "I'll see you at 7:30."

"Okay, tough girl, but dress cool. We have a six-hour drive to Clarksdale, Mississippi where we'll set up base. Parchman is about a thirty minute drive from there. Tomorrow is Friday and Jim told me that visits to inmates are allowed on weekends. I don't think we can get in unless we're family or legal advisors, but Jim Harris said he would call the warden to seek permission for us to talk with Jones. I'll call the prison to arrange to see Jones, if he'll even see us."

"If they'll even let us in," she said.

TWENTY-SEVEN

Morning came too soon but the breakfast buffet was passing good: biscuits and gravy for me, an apple and juice for Sue. We were dressed for the day ahead. Sue had on white short-shorts and a Sweetwater button-front tee, hanging loosely, flip flops and a Panama hat with a choke collar tie fitting under her chin. I wore my khaki shorts and Salty Dog tee, Twins cap and my NBs. By mid afternoon I expected to be in Clarksdale.

We cut off of I-40 onto US 49 and wound through the last hills of Arkansas, through the attractive communities of West Helena and then Helena. Antique shops and beautiful homes lined themselves along the street and then we were across the Mississippi River into the state of Mississippi.

The Delta is unlike any other place in America. From the river, looking east as far as the eye can see is probably the flattest piece of real estate in the United States. The climate is hot and humid, the earth a rich reddish brown, perfect for cotton and soybeans, with an occasional catfish farm popping up along the way. This early afternoon felt like one hundred degrees with equal humidity. The Miata's top was up for now. The air conditioner was the only way to battle the wet atmosphere.

Sue looked at me as we turned on Highway 61, south to Clarksdale. "We're not in Kansas anymore," she said.

"Nope."

"We're not in Colorado anymore either."

"Nope."

"Birmingham at least has hills with twists and turns. This road looks as if it goes on forever."

"Yep."

She looked at me hard. "Are you playing with my mind?"

"Gotta have a mind to play that game," I said.

Rib jab . . . hard.

"The home of the Blues, the true American music," I said a while later. "Muddy Waters and Robert Johnson played here. Their music comes right out of the earth and into your soul. I have a CD of Mississippi Fred McDowell playing the slide guitar. 'Baby Please Don't Go' is classic Delta Blues. I believe it's in slot number five," I said.

Sue turned the radio on, pushed slot five on the CD changer and there was Mississippi Fred McDowell. Outside was the Delta. Inside was the Blues. It gave me goose bumps.

"This music really puts the beauty of the Delta into rightful perspective," she said.

"Hoped you'd think so. I'm ready to put the top down. How about you?"

"Okay."

We stopped and I unsnapped the top. Sue took the honors of raising it up and over our heads and into the roof well.

God, it was hot. But we delighted in the heat now, sweat and all. This was the South.

Clarksdale was home to the Delta Blues Museum and as we traveled down State Street looking for lodging, I told Sue we'd have to try the Ground Zero Blues Club for supper that night down on Blues Alley, next door to the museum.

We found a Comfort Inn. Sue and I went up to the front desk and met Sherille, the desk clerk, who said to us, "Hi y'all. Welcome to Clarksdale. How can I help y'all?"

I said, "We'd like two rooms, nonsmoking, one bed, two nights, and one person in each room."

"Yes sir," she said. "We have just what y'all are lookin' for raught here."

I gave her my credit card. She ran it through, and before you knew it, Sue and I had rooms 114 and 115, directly across the hall from one another. I asked Sue which room she preferred and without hesitation she took the key to room 114. I wondered what went through her head when I asked that. Why would it matter which room one had since the rooms were across the hall from one another? But she appeared adamant and I was too smart to ask.

We parted, agreeing to meet later for supper.

It was 4:00. In my room, I threw my bag on the bed and found a phone book. The call to Parchman got me to the warden's secretary who put me through to the warden. Jim Harris had called and arrangements were made for me for a half hour visit with Mac Jones tomorrow at 1:00. Jones might see me. There were no promises of conversation on his part however. I asked about Sue. She could wait for me in the visitors' room outside the cellblock area, I was told.

There was a knock on my door. Sue came in and looked around. "Nice place you have here. Been gone long, sailor?"

"It's been a long dry spell for this old ship's buzzard. You know. 'Water, water everywhere nor any drop to drink.'"

Sue plopped herself on a chair next to the air conditioner and let the cool air blow over her. "Did you get hold of the prison?"

I filled her in. "And I have a one o'clock visitation with Jones, if he'll see me and there are no promises that even if he sees me he'll talk."

"And me?"

"I'm sorry. Apparently I'm the only one with permission to go in. I asked about you. The warden told me there's a visitor's area you can sit in and wait till I'm done."

She seemed disappointed.

"Sue," I continued, "you weren't exactly scheduled to be with me on this trip, remember?"

"Yes, I know," she said. Her head was down. "Are you sorry I came along?"

"No, no. Not yet. I'm glad you're here. But this is something over which I have no control."

"Okay, I know. It's cool."

It's cool? Talk about your retro-teenage language-arts speak! I really, really liked this girl.

We watched TV for awhile. The Weather Channel's *Local on the 8s* gave an unsavory three day outlook: hot and humid.

Sue left to go clean up for supper. When she returned a short while later, I told her this one was on me. She said only if the next would be her treat.

I agreed.

At six we took off for town. Clarksdale boasted about twenty thousand happy people and with tourists the population was probably twenty two thousand. We parked and walked past the Delta Blues Museum and on into the Ground Zero Blues Club. We sat down and watched the scene play itself out. Most patrons looked like us, tourists waiting to be entertained. According to a chalk board sign at the entrance, the blues band Slow Train was on stage tuning their guitars and reeded clarinets for a night of music. The excitement was electric. We took a look at the menu. The atmosphere was dark and dusky with smoke swirling in the faded lights above the stage. The waitress took our order. Sue zoned in on a Heartbreak Shrimp Sammich, while I favored the Fried Catfish BLT with pickles and seasoned fries on the side. Both of us went for sweet tea to drink. An hour later, the music cried out of lovers lost and left alone. Sue loved it and I got caught up in the feeling. The beer was cold and every one there was a friend.

But it ended all too soon. We went back to the motel and to our rooms, said our goodnights and were off to bed. Tomorrow would be an important day. I had questions, but I knew the nut I had to crack open for the answers was a tough one.

As I lay in bed I thought about the girl across the hall. I reached for the phone. That was stupid. What would I say? Shit. I turned out the light and rolled over for the night.

It was not a restful sleep. I had disjointed dreams of two-by-four inch pines, cigars playing guitars, cotton fields exploding like popcorn in hot oil, Sue driving the Miata into the Mississippi River and out the other side with the top down, carp jumping in and out of the car . . . it went on and on, but the last that woke me was the sight of Josh Holston stepping up to Amy Crenshaw and shooting her in the face multiple times as she lay screaming, "Why, why, why?"

Dying, but never quite dead.

TWENTY-EIGHT

At 5:30 a.m. I was wide awake. I dressed and went to the lounge area of the motel to see if coffee was on. It was. There were donuts and apples on display. CNN blurted out the morning's top news stories to an empty room. I took the coffee, black, a glazed donut and chose an empty table surrounded by four chairs. A *USA Today* lay on the table. I picked it up and turned to the sports section. Baseball had been in full swing. The Twins were thirty-one and twenty, two games back of Chicago. It could be an interesting season. Pitching was good, but there still wasn't that big hitter every other team seemed to enjoy but for Minnesota. They couldn't quite find the resources to pay the big bucks. If they could make it to the all-star break no more than five games back, there might be hope. Oh, where have you gone, Joe DiMaggio?

I looked up and Sue was at the breakfast bar pouring herself a plastic cup of water. She grabbed an apple and headed my way. She sat across from me. She looked tired.

"I'm tired," she said, and took a bite of the apple. "I tossed and turned all night."

"Likewise. You must have a lot on your mind." I liked the way she ate an apple.

"Actually, I think it was the combination of butter-rich shrimp and beer," she looked at me directly.

"Yah, you really went out on the feasting limb last night."

"So what's your excuse, Rick?" she asked.

I didn't like her changing the subject. "Who, me?"

Sue looked slowly around the empty room and then back to me, cocked her head to one side and said, "I don't see any other Rick in this room, Rick."

She was using my own classroom methodology.

"Sorry," I said. "I dreamed dysfunctional dreams last night, the kind with no rhyme or reason."

"Sure, I know about those. And?"

"Say, what about this?" Two could play the changing-subject game. "Let's go to the museum this morning and head for Parchman around noon. Unless you prefer to stay here."

"Say, what about this, he cleverly says." Sue lifted an eyebrow.

I couldn't match her wit, but I bet I could out-wrestle her. I didn't say anything.

"Okay, if you don't want to talk about your dreams, what can a girl like me to do about it? But I will not stay here while you get to have all the fun at the prison."

"Good," I said. "Let's get ready and sight-see this morning before it gets too hot. I imagine you're missing your morning runs."

"You're telling me." She stretched her legs out, looking critically at them.

I looked at her legs too. They looked pretty good. "I'll see you in an hour," I said.

"Roger, Wilko and out," she said.

The museum, when we arrived there later, represented the Delta and the Blues with pride.

TWENTY-NINE

Highway 49 is flat to the point of convex. Highway 49 west took us to Parchman. Along the road, signs read, DO NOT PICK UP HITCHHIKERS. We knew we were close. Then we were there. Arching over the entrance, in broad letters the sign MISSISSIPPI STATE PENITENTIARY proclaimed itself to us and we drove up to the designated parking area, the car tires crunching over a gravel roadway to a cautious stop.

Sue walked with me into a reception area. She found a waiting room with magazines spread over a conference table surrounded by plastic chairs, where she quietly made herself busy reading.

I was directed down a hallway which led to what was the visitors' staging area. There I was ID'd, frisked and put into a common room with other visitors. The room was separated down the middle by a glass wall with chairs on either side, phones for speaking into, and there was a place for me. I sat and was told to wait.

I watched as prisoners came through a door on the opposite side, each finding a familiar face and going to that place. There were mothers, children, girlfriends, obvious lawyers (suits and briefcases) and me.

The chair opposite me remained empty. My mind had envisioned what Mac Jones might look like. I thought about Homer's *Odyssey*, when Odysseus went to the land of the Cyclops. The Cyclops had been warned of Odysseus' coming and had expected a monster of his own size to do battle with but was surprised that Odysseus was a mere mortal, a man, small and weak when compared to the gods. And so I expected to see a one-eyed giant, a slobbering fiend, a merciless monster that would break through the glass and eat me for lunch.

But Mac Jones was not the fiendish ogre I had imagined. I saw a man not so unlike myself come through a doorway. I'd expected green mucous drooling from his mouth and talons where his nails should be. He was just a man, about five-foot ten and he might have weighed 160 pounds dripping wet. He was slightly hunched at the back with thinning brown hair and a brown walrus mustache that nearly made him a comic character, but I kept my personal amusement to myself. He sauntered over to face me, pulled out the chair and dropped into it. He picked up the phone, legs outstretched, arms folded in a mock defensive gesture across his chest with the phone receiver braced between shoulder and chin, and he stared at me.

The ball was obviously in my court.

I started. "I'm Rick Burns and I'm from Colorado."

No response.

"I'm a teacher and I had a student named Josh Holston. Three weeks ago Josh shot and killed two of his fellow classmates."

No response.

"The two kids dated one another. The boy was black, the girl was white."

The right side of his lip moved slightly toward a sneer, barely perceptible, but other than that, no response.

"I spoke with Josh Holston in jail," I continued. "FTNF was a part of that conversation."

No response.

"Josh gave no explanation for what he did to his two fellow classmates."

No response.

"Josh is dead."

Jones just stared at me.

"I went to Garden City, Kansas to talk with Terry Sims. Instead I met Terry's Uncle Eugene. Terry died in an auto accident a few weeks back."

Eyes lifted slightly to my face, but no response.

"I want to know if you knew Josh Holston and whether he was a member of FTNF."

Jones moved slightly and said, "Y'all's a fuckin' Yankee. Wha' the fuck y'all wan' with meh?"

Shit. I could feel my blood begin to boil. I had to settle down. *Be nice*, I told myself.

"I want to know what the hell you did to that boy, Mr. Jones, to make him want to kill innocent people," I said. So much for being nice.

"Mista' Jones is it?" he sneered. "Well here's the anseh. Fuck you, Yank! Wha' that there boy done up in Coloradah was good. No nig'eh has a claim on any white brutha' or sistah in this whole damn world. A nig'eh and a white woman? Man that's wha' this fight's all 'bout. Don y'all know nothin'? And it'll nev'eh be finished till the last nig'eh is dead."

Jones stopped, took a breath, but he wasn't finished. He slammed the phone against the glass and pounded both fists on the counter in front of him and the diatribe continued. He spewed poison at me, the words bouncing off the walls of the bleak room. The guards were on Jones in seconds, pulling him away from the desk and from the room. His fists were still shaking toward me as they dragged him away. The echo of his hate lingered. Other visitors and even the inmates there (most of whom were black) cringed and stared at Jones.

A guard had likewise come to escort me out. He said, "You found yourself a rough one there. He's pretty hardcore."

I found Sue and, without a word, we walked straight to the car. I could tell she had questions, but she remained silent until I was ready to share my experience. Once back on the road toward Clarksdale, I filled her in on what had happened.

"Wow," she said when I paused for breath. "So, nothing learned from this Jones fellow? I'm sorry."

"Actually," I turned toward her. "I learned two things. FTNF is for real and it's dangerous. Two things I *didn't* learn is the extent of Josh Holston's connection with FTNF and how to deal with it. There has to be more to it than those two crazies, Jones and Sims. If FTNF is still active, and I believe it must be, there's someone or some group of people leading the day-to-day affairs."

I pulled off the road outside Rome, checked the signal strength on my phone and called Jim Harris. It was stifling hot outside and the car's air conditioning labored to keep Sue and me comfortable while idling in neutral.

The call was short-lived, and we were on our way again.

"Jim has another name for us to consider," I said. "Jones has a brother named Sam. He lives in Greenwood. His name came up on a criminal register. Sam Jones has served time for stealing cars. According to the records, Jim says he's out of jail and works in a lumber mill north of Greenwood. I have a plan."

We were back in Clarksdale. Sue reminded me that it would be her treat for supper tonight. I didn't argue.

"I'll check out the local dining menus and get back to you in ten minutes," she said.

I was suddenly hungry. "We'll talk plans over dinner."

"Okay. Let me get the prison dust washed off. I felt uncomfortable in that place."

"There's a lot of discomfort at Parchman," I said.

In my room I washed off, but didn't get rid of the image of pure hatred had that contorted Mac Jones' face in that visitors' chamber. Chamber was the wrong choice of words. There was another deadlier 'chamber' at Parchman that belies description.

Sue called in nine minutes. "We're dining at the Rest Haven Restaurant in one hour. Prepare yourself for Kibbie."

"What? "

"Never you mind, Mr. Burns. You don't have to know everything."

An hour and fifteen minutes later I discovered that Kibbie was a very nice mixture of ground round, cracked wheat, olive oil, onions and other secret seasonings. I ordered the Kibbie Burger with pine nuts. Sue ventured for baked Kibbie and stuffed grape leaves. Two sweet teas rounded out the main course.

The restaurant was packed and it was loud, the hustle and bustle of waitresses taking orders and delivering food, the busboys clearing tables, the sounds of silverware and glass gathered and placed in tubs on carts, rolled off to the kitchen where, when the doors opened, you could hear the cooks and staff barking orders for grill use, the dishwashers working to full capacity, all of it looking like chaos but running like clockwork.

It was swell eating. Dessert seemed to be a part of the meal, and I didn't argue sharing a piece of chocolate cream pie topped with a meringue that stretched from here to the moon. Sue did her part. I was proud. I was full! Sue's smile as she looked about the room and at me eased the burden of what I had to say next.

Over a final sweet tea I told her of my plan.

"I'm still not sure how this is going to pan out, but I want to do serious harm to FTNF," I said. "Going to Mac Jones and asking outright did not score any points. We need to be quiet about discovery as it relates to FTNF. If this Sam Jones is involved, I don't want him to know I'm a threat to his organization. I just don't think he'd be very cooperative."

"So, what do you intend?" asked Sue.

"I intend to find this Sam, follow him till he leads me to FTNF. Then I will simply deal with the organization, figuratively speaking that is."

Sue was persistent. "And just how will you do that?"

"I haven't thought about how, but it'll happen."

"Rick," she said, "this sounds a little dangerous to me. It sounds like someone could get hurt."

"Someone already has been hurt. Things have changed, Sue."

Her smile disappeared.

"This feeling of whatever it is I need to do has taken on a life of its own. It's an uncomfortable change. And you are going home."

"What did you just say?"

"Sue, I don't know what will happen. Because it might be dangerous, I don't want anything to happen to you."

"So what do you propose to do? Toss me in a corner, tell me to stay and be good till you come back? That is *if* you come back at all, in some glorified honor of having revenged yourself for Bob and Amy? It's all about revenge now, isn't it? If that's the case, then you can take a flying leap. I can give as well as take. Is it because I'm a woman? I'm probably in better physical shape than you and I think you just might need me to watch out for things that go bump in the night."

I wasn't in a listening mood and continued as if she'd said nothing.

"I'll pack you up tomorrow morning and you'll drive the

Miata back to Colorado. I'm going to rent a car here in Clarksdale and take it to Greenwood. I'll rent a vehicle that blends in to the surroundings. The Miata would stick out like a sore thumb. I'll find Jones in Greenwood and follow him till I find what I'm looking for. When I'm through in Mississippi, I'll see you back home."

"Did you not hear me?" Sue asked. Her lips were curled back like a panther's. "I don't care about the danger. I'm here for the duration. I don't cut and run." She leaned toward me. "You took me on. I admit I didn't give you much of a choice in the matter, but I'll be darned if I'm going to give you the satisfaction of 'protecting the poor little girl' in this affair. Right now I don't like you very much, Mr. Burns."

"I did hear you, but I don't like it," I said. "I don't know how long it'll take and I don't know what danger there might be. I don't understand the force that's driving me right now. Whatever it is, Sue, it has a single intention and personal safety be damned."

She sensed an opening and went for it. "You are stuck with me, Rick, like glue to paper. Thanks for the concern, but I'm a big girl. What happens, happens. If there is fault it won't be yours to own up to, it'll be mine. Besides, I wouldn't be able to stand it if you got hurt and I wasn't there to help. You have no right to put that burden on me."

Sue had by now moved her chair close to mine and I could feel her breath on my face as she spoke. Her perfume drifted through me, her hands found mine and clenched tight. I felt some primal urge to either slap her insubordinate face or kiss her right there, chocolate pie, meringue and all.

The people around us seemed oblivious to our conversation, but the waitress was coming our way with the check. I looked at Sue as she was about to continue her case, and motioned to her that the waitress was there. She moved back in her seat, took out a credit card, offering it to the waitress without looking up, not moving her eyes from mine.

I knew the fight was over and she was going to stay. I could have out-muscled her for honor's sake. She wasn't so tough. Then again, maybe she was.

The check was signed, tip was left, and so did we.

At the car, I said, "Okay, you make a valid point. I am humbled by your resolute desire to keep going through this with me. But at least it's been said. There are unknowns out there and we may not like what we find. If you're certain about it, then okay."

"Thank you," she said as she opened the door and got into the Miata.

"Thank you for supper," I said. "It was very good, and the company was above average . . . considering."

I was in the car, releasing the brake when Sue put her hand on mine.

"I'll be alright, Rick Burns. You're a gentleman, which makes you more of a man than you might think."

I don't remember much of the drive back to the motel. I was busy plugging several holes in the fence.

THIRTY

Sundays are not usually the best day to conduct business, but I managed to find a car rental agency open for tourist trade and found a self-storage garage complex to keep the Miata safe until our return. Our choice of vehicle was a white, older model Chevy Impala, with Mississippi plates. That was the nice thing about local rental agencies: the only vehicles in stock are generally older models. Add to that the fact that there were only three models from which to choose and they were all older model white Chevys. Sue and I looked fairly harmless as we pulled out onto Highway 49 and off to Greenwood, an hour or so drive away.

It was another day in the Delta with the kind of heat that rose out of the ground. Even the grass radiated hot and clammy.

"Even Birmingham isn't this kind of hot," Sue said after we had started.

"That brings up something I wanted to ask you," I said.

"Sure. What?"

"Did you go to a public or private school in Birmingham?"

Sue looked sideways at me. The Impala afforded us the luxury of distance that the Miata didn't, but I caught the full brunt of her stare.

"My parents sent me to public schools K-12. I never regretted it. I had friends in private schools. We just did our thing after school or on weekends. If you're hinting about the racial issue, there was much of that, mostly unspoken.

"The South still resists integration. Some people just can't get over the Civil War. Sure, it's subtle compared to what it used to be, but it's there. My parents raised me to be aware of racism. They taught me to embrace diversity rather than reject it.

"When I started my freshman year, I was given the choice to

attend either public or private school. It was an easy decision. I cultivated friends both black and white and that was just the way it was. It seemed ridiculous that I would want to change the way things had been. I will forever be grateful to my parents for raising me the way they did and for giving me the freedom of choice when I was young. Now does that answer your nosey little question, Mr. Burns?"

"You knew I was going to ask it," I said. "One more question."

"Fire away."

"Will it ever get better?"

"In my honest opinion, many in the South hang on to what they refer to as tradition and heredity, as they say. These are false tenants. Tradition, if it treated humans inhumanly, is bad tradition. Heredity, when argued, begs the question, what heredity? If it is one that enslaved and isolated, then there is no source of pride there, thank you very much. However, those are the two most arguable points many bring on to bolster their views and to continue to discriminate against their fellow human beings. I simply will not be that way.

"You can't change some people's hearts, Rick. I believe we are still more animal than human in many regards. It makes me sick sometimes. And don't think subtle racism is lost on minorities. They are quite aware, and many throw it right back at us. And so it does no one any good in the end. I only can say once more that I won't be that way."

"You must love your mom and dad," I said.

"I do."

"Me too."

THIRTY-ONE

At the junction of Highways 49 and 8 I headed east. We drove over the Tallahatchie River. Sue noticed the sign.

"So we're on the Tallahatchie Bridge," she said as she looked out the side window, over the railing and at the river below. "It sure is a dirty river. I remember the Bobbie Gentry song, 'Ode to Billie Joe.' That was back in the sixties, wasn't it? Do you think Billie Joe MacAllister is down there? I don't think we'd find him in that brown goo."

"Or Emmett Till," I added.

"Emmett Till. Where have I heard that name before?"

"Another senseless murder, like the Clutter family, where human beings once again proved themselves unable to act humanely."

We had turned south on Cr-518, and with the Tallahatchie River on our right and flat farmland to the left, we came to the small town of Money. I pulled over onto the gravel shoulder next to the Illinois Central Railroad which runs parallel to the road.

Sue looked at me. "Are you throwing me out? You could have asked first. I won't go easily."

"Don't tempt me, Ms. Richy," I said.

"So what's up? Do you think money is going to fall from some tree, here in Money?" She was getting a real kick out of herself.

"Look over at the town there," I said, pointing to the west. "What do you see?"

"Well," she said, "I see a street lined with buildings on one side and a railroad on the other and some houses off further behind, to the west."

"Very good," I said. "Now direct your attention to the building I'm pointing at."

I aimed my right arm straight out perpendicular to the car across Sue's face and rubbed her nose teasingly with the sleeve of my shirt.

She hit my arm with her left hand and said, "That's what used to be a business of some kind but has obviously failed. All that's left are four walls, a boarded-up doorway and windows, and a second level where the roof has fallen in. I would hazard to guess that no one is home. Rick. Why are you asking me about this building in this town? I'm beginning to worry about you again."

"Well, my little chickadee," I said. "That building represents perhaps the most popular notion of the beginning of what we today call the Civil Rights Movement, the movement that culminated with the passage of the Civil Rights Bill of 1965, thank you, President Johnson."

"What?" she asked.

"It was into that building back in the early 1950s that Emmett Till walked one day. Till was a fourteen-year-old black boy from Chicago, who'd come to visit his uncle, Mose Wright. Till did not understand the rules of the South. He acted out a dare from friends and talked to or whistled at—no one knows for certain—a white lady who worked in that very building which was then called Bryant's Grocery and Meat Market. When his friends realized what he had done, they made him run away. The white woman in the store was Carolyn Bryant, the wife of Roy Bryant, the owner. Long story short, Till's body was found floating in the Tallahatchie River, not far from where you and I were a few minutes ago. The boy's body was so disfigured as to be unrecognizable. He'd been beaten and shot and many days under water. At his funeral, the casket remained opened, as his mother insisted. And the reason why?"

"'So the world could see what they did to my boy,'" said Sue. "Till's mother was a guest on *Oprah* several years ago. I remember that those were her words."

"*Jet* magazine carried the pictures exclusively. The world saw the ugly face of racism, and the rest of the country began to realize that something was not quite right down south."

"Wasn't there a trial?"

"Yah, Roy Bryant and another white man were accused and there was a trial of sorts," I said. "Many referred to it as a circus. Mississippi justice was different from real justice. No white jury would convict a white of killing a black in Mississippi in the fifties.

"But Mose Wright was a brave man. He was the star witness for the prosecution. He stood up at that trial, and in front of a sea of white faces, he identified Bryant and the other man as the two who took his nephew away in the middle of a night. And Emmett Till disappeared into history."

"And this building?" Sue asked.

"Is all that's left. I personally like to think that it's been allowed to rot as a symbol of how the Civil Rights Movement beat down racism, at least in the eyes of the laws of the land."

"But the hearts of some will never change," she said.

"And I know now that that's why I'm here and maybe why you're here too?"

"Are we going to change some hearts?" she asked.

"Or break some laws trying," I replied.

THIRTY-TWO

We came into the north end of Greenwood, and I found the way back to Highway 82 and a Hampton Inn. It had a continental breakfast and a front desk manager, Jim Bob. I asked Jim Bob for two rooms, nonsmoking, one bed, one night to start and one person in each room. He said, "Yes Sir." He took my card and made a copy while I signed in for the rooms. Jim Bob hoped I would enjoy my stay and told us that the complimentary hot breakfast would be ready at 5:30 a.m. Per instructions, I gave Sue a copy of the billing when I came back to the car.

"How did it go?" she asked.

"The manager has two first names."

"It happens in the South."

"And there's a complimentary hot breakfast," I said.

"That's nice," she said.

"One bad thing, though."

"And that would be?"

"No pets allowed."

"Meaning?"

"I'll sneak you in but you'll have to lie low."

Rib jab.

We took the elevator to the second floor. I gave Sue the key for the room closest to the fire escape. She gave me the kind of look that said, "You're learning."

I opened her door for her and said, "It's five o'clock, there's a pool and we really have nothing to do till tomorrow. I'll call Jim Harris in a bit. He said he'd fax a picture of Sam Jones to us when we found where we'd be staying. That's when the fun starts."

"A swim sounds good," she said, and walked into her room.

I changed into my bright yellow, knee-length oversized trunks. The motel towel was of good water-absorbent quality and I barefooted it outside.

The heat was oppressive and the pool water was only a tad bit wetter than the outside air. The pool itself was of moderate size with a shallow and deep end.

There were five children, ranging in ages between what looked like three and seven, screaming and splashing at the shallow side. Moms and dads were alternately in or out of the pool, playing Frisbee or tossing beach balls to the little ones. I noticed that sunscreen was liberally and often applied to the little ones.

Then Sue was there, and all eyes turned toward her. Dads stopped throwing Frisbees as she walked past the shallow end of the pool, holding her towel in one hand, casual and at ease. She was wearing a chocolate-colored one-piece suit, a cross back spaghetti-strapped thing with a dipped neckline and low-cut legs.

Her layered auburn hair fell down about her shoulders, and her blue eyes sparkled. I was in the water, and while she walked along the pool's edge I swam over to get a better look. I was like an adolescent kid hanging on to the side of the pool, arms latched together, watching, no, staring at the most beautiful woman I'd ever seen. Sue looked like a daughter of Zeus come to earth to save the lost soul of some poor mortal. That would be me. The sun behind her added an aura of light that intensified the image. Her legs, tanned and sturdy, were a hurdler's legs; her arms had form and shape that bespoke strength. The whole package was fluid motion and very easy on the eyes.

Sue tossed her towel over mine, kicked off her sandals and, without a word, walked over to where I was, placed her foot firmly on my head and pushed. I fell backwards into the deep water. Sue dove in and was beside me. I kicked once, and with both hands, found the top of her head and took her down to eight feet under. She pushed up from the bottom and both of us broke the surface, laughing and fighting, hands slapping water at one another like kids. After a few side strokes around the deep end of the pool, more dips and splashes, we found the ladder, picked up our towels and patted off the excess water. I dragged two lounge chairs to the table and we sat, stretching our legs out to let the late afternoon sun do its thing.

"Nice suit, Wilbert. Where are your shoes?" Sue asked.

"I came bare-naked below the knees." I nodded toward the moms at the shallow end and said, "Thought I'd give the ladies a cheap thrill."

"You have part of that right," she said.

"The part about the thrill?"

"The part about cheap."

"You're not nice."

"Why, thank you, Mr. Burns," she returned. "That was my intention."

"But you look okay for a girl,"

Sue looked me in the eye and said, in a softer tone, "I try."

I looked away. *Rick, what is happening to you? Get hold of yourself. There is no good in this. There is hurt. Don't go there!*

The families at the other end of the pool left and it was just the two of us. With the kids gone it was silent around the pool. Evening insects were beginning to make their presence known. A train in the distance whistled a warning as it tracked through town. I believed it was actually starting to cool a bit. I felt stronger now. The old feelings had passed. I was hoping, and this would be a nice night, so, *carpe* it. Tomorrow should bring good things if I could just persuade myself of it.

On the walked back to our rooms I turned to Sue. "Are you tired of Southern fare?"

"Not a bit! I love the food, and I miss the South at times like these. We used to swim every day back home when I was growing up. So, where do you want to eat this time?"

"Your choice tonight. Something Southern."

"Okay then," she said. "Southern Sonic."

"Sonic?"

"Sonic."

"Meet you at the car," I said.

We found a Sonic and parked to deliver our order. There's nothing quite like Southern Sonic toaster sandwiches, Coneys and Strawberry Cream Slushies.

As we finished off our slushies under the trademarked

canopy, I said, "Wasn't Sonic actually an Oklahoma idea?"

"Oklahoma is the South. And some of the Sonic ideas came from even farther south. The idea for the intercom speakers? That came from Louisiana. That ties Sonic, in fact, to the Deep South." Sue glowered at me.

I saw I'd touched a nerve and decided to take full advantage of the situation.

"If I'm not mistaken, isn't Waffle House more of a complete southern idea? Wouldn't that have been a better choice?"

She gave me a discerning look. "Waffle House comes from Georgia. Say, I'm surprised and very impressed by your gastronomic knowledge, but let's not split hairs on this issue, Mr. Burns."

With that she reached over and a finger-painting of strawberry slush was applied to my face. What I owed Sue Richy in payback was beginning to add up. I would just keep an active running tab for her in my mind.

THIRTY-THREE

The fax from Jim Harris came in next morning at eight. I went down to the desk to pick it up, signed for another night's stay and called Sue's room from there, telling her that I'd be in the lounge with coffee and fruit and a picture of Sam Jones and wouldn't she like to come join me.

The breakfast lounge opened up from the main lobby through a hallway flanked by a mirrored wall. I checked out the day's attire: Lee jeans and Bronco's tee, New Balance shoes but no socks. Just another tourist. I sat at a small, two-chaired table near a secondary exit leading to the pool. Two of the dads and two of the children from yesterday's swimming party were at the other end of the lounge making waffles and picking sausage and bacon by the tongs-full, piling gravy on biscuits, drinking orange juice, eating cereal and two percent milk, sharing toast with peanut butter and jelly and snarfing down donuts, all while watching cartoons on the in-house television. It was disgusting. I was jealous.

I sat and looked face-to-face at Sam Jones, via the picture that Jim had faxed. Sam had been cut from his brother's genetic pattern, only older by ten years. The picture was a full-face police photo. His hair, like his brother's, was thinning, only more so; his eyes were gray and narrow-set, the nose hawkish. The smile was a sneer. I had seen that smile before, but in Sam Jones there was a toothless space where two central incisors should have been. The cheeks were sallow. The information on age and height was found on page two along with his rap sheet: fifty years old, five-foot eleven-inches tall and divorced. He was definitely a small-crime man, but he was consistent: petty theft, check forgery, trespassing, DWI, and carrying a gun while in the act of a larceny. That got my attention. I read on. The gun hadn't been loaded, but Sam Jones had been. He'd mistaken a Coke machine for an ATM at a shopping center on the north end of town and had threatened the device with a .357 Baretta. That event had earned him six months in the Sunflower County Jail.

Sam Jones was also a card-carrying member of FTNF.

A side note from Jim indicated that gun ownership laws were quite lax in Mississippi, and to be careful down there with whatever it was I was trying to do. If a man had one gun he'd probably have two or more at home. Guns were easy to get in Mississippi, at trade shows or on the streets. According to the present laws, no gun permits were necessary in Mississippi, and there were no private sale background checks in Mississippi.

Sue came to the table, ready for the day in tan shorts and a pine-green Bella scooped-neck tank top and a pair of Nike trainers, with socks. Once again, eyes went to her as she passed.

Sue stood next to me, looking at my plate. "Didn't you say coffee and fruit? All I see there is coffee and a donut."

"It's a blueberry donut," I said.

She opened-handed the back of my head and went to the buffet, returning with a dry, toasted bagel and orange juice.

Sue sat down across the table from me, took the fax and read through the entire document while munching on the bagel and sipping orange juice.

After she'd finished reading, Sue looked at me and said, "This Sam isn't very bright, but he looks dangerous and I don't like the gun business. Perhaps we should talk about this a little more, Rick."

I ignored her. "I think we'll check out his home address and work address. I noticed a saw mill when we drove in on Money Road yesterday. That must be his workplace. It fits the description. I checked the phone book last night and found his home address." I reached into my wallet and brought out a page of motel notepaper with an address on it. "It's outside of town, not far off Highway 82. Let's drive there first and see what we find. Or you can stay here."

"You're the boss, Boss," she said. "I'll be with you."

I noted sarcasm.

"I can whip your butt, you know," I said.

"I know," she said.

"Just so we're straight on that. I dunked you four times in the pool yesterday," I reminded her.

"Why, yes, you did, didn't you?" Sue smiled, stood and walked out.

I watched her disappear to the elevator. "Shit!" I said a little too loudly.

I looked around the lounge. One of the little swimmer kids at the far table called out to his father, "That man said 'shit,' Daddy!"

All eyes turned, but I had already slipped out the side exit.

THIRTY-FOUR

Sue was waiting at the rental car. I admired her stubborn resistance, which seemed to be the dominant part of her character.

It was a day like most, hot and humid. Traffic was light and directions straightforward: Highway 82 west to Sand Creek Road and north to box number 342. Sand Creek Road was an oil-based road. The drive took ten minutes, and less than a mile off 82 we saw 342, set in front of a simple ranch house with a porch running across the front, door in the center. There was no garage, but there was a tin-roofed carport set apart about forty feet from the house.

An older model, red Ford F-150 was in the port, a squirrel rifle hanging on a rack inside the back window.

I drove past the house, turned onto a grass lane that led off the oiled road, disappearing into a grove of river birch. I stopped.

"He might be home," I said. "Let's take a position that'll allow us a clear view of the truck yet keep us out of direct sight from the house."

"Yes, sir." Sue sat up straight, surveying the landscape. No sarcasm in that; no hint of anything other than strict affirmation.

I backed the car onto the oil road and inched toward the view I needed. I eased it to the far side of the road and stopped, rolled the windows down and turned off the engine. We were in shade, yet had a clear vision of the truck.

Little traffic moved on this desolate road and for the first half hour there was nothing. Then we heard the sound of a springed screen door creak and slam shut. Two figures walked toward the truck. They were too far away to identify but by the stature either could have been Sam Jones.

They got in the truck. The engine fired and it moved out of

the carport onto Sand Creek Road, turning toward Highway 82.

I looked over at Sue and said, "Ready or not here we go."

We moved out ourselves and followed at what I considered a safe distance. The truck traveled toward Greenwood, catching Money Road and turning north.

"I hope he's going to work," I said, "so at least we'll know where he lives and works. That way we'll have a base of operations, so to speak."

"How's that?" Sue asked.

"I'd like to have a sense of freedom to do a little exploring in his house when he's not there."

She didn't look too thrilled at this.

The truck traveled three miles north of town and turned at a sign which read Cheever's Lumber Mill. I kept the Impala at a discreet distance. The truck drove up to a wooden structure close to the road with the word OFFICE painted above its entrance. The truck stopped at a horizontal log which had been laid out along a grass lawn bordering the graveled parking area.

I stopped the Impala just short of the business entrance, while we were still close enough to identify the occupants of the truck as they exited.

The driver matched the picture of Sam Jones. The rider was a younger man, in his late teens or early twenties. They both went inside the building.

Sue asked, "Now what?"

"Now would be that time when I had a plan. Give me a minute. Let's make sure that those two are here to stay for a while."

Minutes later, both men emerged from the office, walked across the parking lot and disappeared behind an outer building.

We waited for a few minutes. A fully-loaded Mack logging truck came from the back lot and parked in front of the office. Jones and his friend stepped out of the truck and walked back into the office. They were out in less than a minute and back in the truck, which they drove out the main entrance right past our vehicle, turning south.

Sue and I had hastily ducked down. We were low in the seat, head-to-head, close to the floor and invisible. After the sound of the truck faded away, we rose and faced one another, relieved and sweating just a little.

"I should have found a better spot," I said.

"At least in this car we aren't sticking out like a sore thumb," she said.

"Yah. Well, it appears they're on a run to somewhere and may be gone a while, but just to be sure . . ." I reached for my cell phone and dialed the phone number printed on the Cheever's Lumber Mill sign.

The call was picked up after two rings.

"Cheever's Mill, Jed here."

"Jed, this is John Sans from Delta Cable." I used my best southern drawl without exploiting it beyond proportion. "We're looking for a Sam Jones about his cable hook-up. Is this his work number?"

"Yah, Sam works here. He's out on a run to Greenwood right now. But I got his home number here somewhere. Just a minute."

A minute went on by and Jed came back. "You there?"

"Yah, Jed."

"Number's 555-4792."

"Got it. Thanks a lot." I hung up. "That was easy," I said. "Now for the plan."

Sue looked at me with child-like eyes.

"Let's head back to the Jones house and take a peak around; see what there is to see, look for anything FTNF."

We drove back to Sand Creek Road and turned onto the same grass lane as before but further off the road, hiding the Impala in the birch grove. We got out of the car and, staying inside the tree line, made our way back to the house.

The temperature was hovering at ninety-five degrees and ninety percent humidity. My shirt was soaked just stepping out of the car and walking fifty yards. A short clearing between the grove and the house made us vulnerable to the view of road traffic. There was none, so we sprinted the thirty yards to the back door. Sue was fast and it was all I could do to keep up with her. She looked at me when we were at the door. My heavy panting gave me away. She was barely breathing, but said nothing. I'm sure she filed this experience away for future use.

The back door was screened, but the screen was not locked. I looked around to the front of the house to check for life. It was all quiet on the western front. I returned to Sue at the back door.

"Looks like it's just you and me," I said. "Here's where we start breaking the law. You can back out anytime and I'll understand."

Sue gave me a conspiratorial look and opened the door herself.

We slipped into a kitchen, which was more of a galley with room enough for one to operate. A fridge, stove, a sink filled with dirty dishes, a microwave, a wall telephone and three cabinets hanging on the walls. The kitchen opened to a small area with a dinette table and two chairs, which in turn opened to a living area that held a black vinyl couch, a maple coffee table adorned with *Hustler* and *Playboy* mags and five empty Buds, and a beanbag chair plopped in front of a twenty-five inch Magnavox which was perched on an empty box crate. At least it was hooked up to cable. On one wall was a black plastic-framed poster of the Confederate Navy Jack, the symbol of the South. Most northerners refer to it as the Southern Cross or Stars and Bars. Something about this flag in this room in this house where there probably lived a practicing racist anarchist, twisted this symbol of pride into a desecration. What other human violations rested here? The windows were covered by white generic blinds. The outside road ran by some one hundred feet away.

Sue picked up one of the *Hustler* mags and laughed. "At least they're literate."

"I'm sure they have them just for the articles," I said.

She opened the magazine, said, "*E-w-w*," and dropped it back on the table.

A hallway led from the living room to a bathroom at the far end, flanked by two bedrooms. There was nothing particularly noteworthy about these rooms other than they were small with closets built to perspective. Each had a single bed and dresser and one window; the walls were bare. The bath was tiled with what had once been white faux marble porcelain tiles. There was a shower, a single sink and commode. The floors throughout the house were wood-planked with a few braided area rugs, all falling apart at the seams.

The house showed no evidence of a woman's touch.

Sue asked, "What next?"

"I think you should get a vacuum cleaner, a dust rag, a mop, soap and water and get to work."

"Only if I die first," she said.

"Hey, I'm just trying to give you purpose here."

"Rick . . ." The eyebrows arched and the head tilted to one side. The mouth was serious.

"Okay. Let's pick a room and look for anything that might clue us in to FTNF. Start with the bedrooms and work out to the kitchen. Keep one ear open for trouble from the outside." Then I added, "You, of course, will start with the room closest to the exit."

I couldn't help myself.

She took a swing and missed. I had already gone into the farther of the two bedrooms.

The closet was clean except for a couple of tee-shirts on hangers, a pair of jeans, running shoes and a belt on the floor. The bed and mattress were clean and the floor beneath held only dust bunnies. The dresser had three drawers. The two bottom drawers were empty, the top had socks and underwear and a *Soldier of Fortune* magazine.

A computer was set up in the northwest corner of the room on a desk with chair pulled up to it. The screen was dark. I casually moved the mouse with my right hand, and the screen came alive in front of me with a familiar picture: The words "Finished Tasks Need Finishing, The New World Order" in red lettering and the dripping tears of blood beneath the letters "i" in "finished" and "finishing."

"Well, I'll be damned," I murmured.' "This is some kind of wallpaper."

I looked for a password in order to log on but found none.

"Damn!"

I went out to the hallway and into the bathroom. There was nothing suspicious in there; an antihistamine inhaler sat on a shelf. Then I heard Sue exclaim, "What's this?"

"Find something?" I asked.

I walked to the other bedroom and found Sue at the dresser. The second drawer had been pulled out. She was holding a manila folder that appeared to be full of papers. She handed it over.

I took it and peeked inside. "Let's see what we have here, Ms. Richy."

Sue leaned over my shoulder while I opened the folder, pouring its contents on top of the dresser. I dealt the papers out in solitaire fashion, keeping their original order as Sue had found it, and took a long look.

Much of the contents were various dated newspaper clippings from a number of different Mississippi cities. The clippings were of police reports. Certain reports were highlighted in orange. There were other newer clippings also, some with pictures and others with print only. Beside the newspaper items there was a black-covered college-lined notebook. I thumbed through it. The last two-thirds of the notebook were blank, but the first part was filled with pen and pencil notations.

Sue and I looked up in tandem at the sound of a vehicle outside the house. I went to the living room, pressed my back against the wall and sidled up to the window for a look. The vehicle was a tractor. It was pulling a disk. It went on by without turning in to Jones' drive.

This did, however, remind both of us that what we were doing was illegal and probably dangerous.

"Sue," I said. "Would you mind keeping a lookout while I go through these papers?"

"No problem." She went over to the window to keep watch.

I went back to the bedroom where the papers were laid out on the dresser. On closer look, there were four news articles, two of which had accompanying pictures, two other stories with no pics, and there were eight highlighted police reports. The common link in all these were that they all involved arson fires set in churches across western Mississippi. The pictures were of burned and scarred buildings that appeared to be total losses. The police reports were of those same stories.

The last police report had a handwritten notation off to the side that stated, STRAIGHT ON! in large letters. I read through this story:

> Heralding back to the 1960s, the Reverend Jimmy Peers on Thursday morning discovered his church burned to the ground. Some time after five o'clock on Wednesday evening a fire of suspicious origin burned down the Harrington Baptist Church located at 1834 Prospect Road five miles northwest of Tchula. Sheriff Bobby Tulane and the state fire marshal determined arson as the cause. Residue from a crude explosive device was discovered at the rear of the building. This is the fourth church bombing this spring in the Delta. All four bear similar details: All were Baptist churches with predominantly African American congregations; all were arson related as a result of a primitive yet effective combination of chemical fertilizer and diesel fuel with heat ignition; and all bombs were set at points that were farthest from field of vision in order to create optimal destruction. There are no suspects. The sheriff would like anyone with information regarding these bombings to call their local sheriff's department. A reward is offered. This reporter wonders who and why. We thought those days had ended decades ago, but here we go again.

I went back to the notebook and read what was there. There were bits and pieces of rambling thoughts. The jist was racist in nature, not fit to read, and definitely FTNF related. The name 'Charlie Goode' was notated here and there across the pages. Apparently Charlie was the young man with Jones. Charlie couldn't have been any more than eighteen years old, same as Josh. There was mention of what appeared to be a general meeting place. It didn't give an exact location, but somewhere near Winona, Mississippi, was indicated by notes as a place where members met formally.

As I turned the pages I got the notion that FTNF was actively engaged in its original intent: violence through terrorism. Although it didn't come right out and say so, I was fairly certain the church bombings in the articles I had in front of me had originated from FTNF. I needed proof, but it wasn't here. Yet there left little doubt in my mind that Sam Jones was a bad boy. Bad boys need their comeuppance.

"Sue!" I called.

She came into the room. "Well?" she asked.

I showed her the papers, told her about the computer and said, "FTNF is alive and well. But we need to catch these guys in the act."

We put all the papers back as we had found them, and walked from the bedroom back to the living room. There was nothing else out of the ordinary except for what one might find in any bachelor's house: a messy living room and messy kitchen.

Once outside the house, the heat really hit us, and only then did we realize how drained our bodies were.

Before taking the run back to the car, I glanced toward the wooded area behind the house, beyond the carport, and noticed an area of slightly worn grass that led into undergrowth and on into the woods.

"Sue, before we make the dash, I want to check something out," I said.

Sue followed me to the woods. There was some loose brush lying in what was obviously an attempt to cover up a haphazard pathway leading away from the open yard. We followed it and came to a spot about fifty yards into the trees that opened up slightly, where we found a canvas ridge supply tent. It was light brown, blending with its surroundings. It was about nine-by-twelve feet in size and looked to be about six feet at the peak. The whole tent had been erected on top of heavy plastic.

"This is interesting," Sue said.

"More than interesting," I said. "Let's see what's inside."

I walked up to the entrance. The material was first rate and the zipper was of heavy duty. This was no ordinary camping tent; it was of government military quality. Thickly wound canvas tethers secured the tent door. I untied them and zippered the door open. The sound of the zipper was loud and penetrating compared to the quiet surroundings. It was very dark inside. There were no more openings to the outside other than the main flap. It was an eye-adjusting experience. The floor was canvas, like the rest. There was a canvas rise to step over when entering. As my eyes and nose became focused, any further questions I had about FTNF being involved in something quite illegal were put to rest. In one half of the tent were ten bags of what appeared to be some sort of granular chemical fertilizer. In the other half were two red, five-gallon metal drums, and the faint smell of diesel filled the air. In one corner lay three stacks of newspapers wrapped in plastic and, also wrapped in plastic, a half bale of cotton.

I turned to Sue. Her eyes were wide. She mouthed an, "Oh shit," and turned toward the house.

We hadn't realized it, but the thickness of the outside woods had muffled the road sounds and we hadn't heard the truck pull into the drive. Not until it was parked, and we heard the doors slam shut and a voice call out, "Charlie, git the beer in the fridge. I'll be jist a minute."

THIRTY-FIVE

The boys were home early.

I put my forefinger to my lips and ushered Sue to the door flap. I looked back at the scene. We hadn't touched anything inside the tent. But I couldn't zip the flap closed because it would make too much noise. So I unfolded it carefully to cover the opening, tying it shut using a simple shoe tie, as I'd found it when we first got there.

I heard Jones move the brush to the side and begin to walk the path to the tent, toward us. There was no time to spare and nowhere to go without calling attention to our location. We tiptoed around the tent to the back and stood quietly. We were exposed to anyone who might happen along this side of the tent. Our hearts were beating in unison, each breath was labor intensive; sweat pouring down our faces and arms and legs. As Jones approached, I could tell when he stopped at the front flap of the tent. He untied the cords and in that motion must have noticed the zipper opened.

"Goddamn that Charlie," he said.

He stepped inside. We heard him rustling paper and moving bags and he was soon out again. This time Jones zippered the door and tied it down. He began walking around the tent. He stopped within a few steps of where we stood. We held our breaths. He cussed the day and spit. Then we heard him walk away.

Sue and I looked at one another and let out a sighing breath. But the fun wasn't over yet. We needed to get to the car without being seen. We needed to get out of there and we needed to do it immediately.

I looked around to get our bearings, then we headed to the

north from the tent through the trees and heavy brush. It was later afternoon by then. It was slow-going and the mosquitoes were beginning to exercise their rights to our blood. In less than five minutes we reached the lane running from the main road. We jogged back toward the road and soon saw the car nestled among the trees. It appeared to be safe and sound.

Once inside, I turned the ignition and the old Chevy rose to the occasion. I backed it out and went north this time, away from the house. Sand Creek Road went two miles north before turning into Sermon Road. I had no clue which way to turn from there, so flipped the internal coin all males keep in their heads. Left it was. The road turned from oil to gravel. Left may have been a bad choice. But Sermon Road wound around to the south and we eventually made our way back to the main highway.

Once back at the motel we went to my room and drank much water in air conditioned comfort. The room had a worktable with one chair. Sue brought a chair from her room. We sat, iced water in glasses, concession machine food on the table, feeling the cool air blow over our heads, and we talked.

"We need a clear direction," I said. "We have to put this organization to bed for good."

"What about the police, Rick?" she asked.

"I know, I know. We can do that . . . now or later. I think later is better. I need to do this myself."

"You and your guilt?"

"Maybe it's part of that, but I started this and I'll finish it. This isn't finished yet."

She stared at me. "So it isn't just your ego."

"No, it isn't. We destroy FTNF by eliminating it as a functional entity. If we can connect FTNF with the church bombings, implicate the whole organization, and prove that Sam Jones was the leader, I think we'll be able to go home."

I threw a blank look toward Sue, as if I had no ego issues and waited for an argument from her.

She smiled and said, "Let's work to that end, Mr. Burns."

I wished she wouldn't call me that.

"Okay. Now, in the notebook, there was a reference to a meeting tomorrow near Winona. I think we might find out how organized FTNF is and how many practicing members there are. If they're true to their philosophy and if they're bombing churches, they're seriously dangerous. Let's follow these two and see what happens tomorrow.

"Up bright and early then?"

"On the road at six-thirty."

"Okay. If there isn't anything else, I need a shower in a big way." And with that, Sue got up and walked to the door.

I followed. She opened it and turned. I was right there, and she looked slightly up to my face, her eyes a liquid blue and the fragrance of her body was anything but in need of a shower. Her eyes and her scent knocked holes in the fence I couldn't repair fast enough.

For lack of anything better, I said, "You can opt out of tomorrow."

She moved to me and whispered, "I am in this to the end, whatever that end might be, Rick. I'm here for the Joshes and Bobs and Amys of the world, too, just like you. But I'm also here for me, and I'm here for you."

With that, Sue reached her right hand to the side of my neck, running her fingers along my face and then across my mouth, each finger tracing the shape of my lower lip. "Good night, Rick Burns."

She turned and walked out. I heard her open the door to her own room and I listened to the slow close of the door's mechanism and the familiar click of the hardware which secured her room. I looked out. The hallway was empty, the echo of her closing door the only sound.

I turned back in to my room, walked to clothes dresser, leaned my hands on its flat top, looked at the stranger in the framed mirror in front of me and said, "Jumping Jesus, what just happened?"

THIRTY-SIX

Sleep didn't come softly and the morning found me lying in bed on my side, eyes wide open, watching the gray light of dawn filter through the drapery, which hung loosely across the window.

The front desk girl gave a cheery hello when I walked past for coffee and inquired how my night had gone. I gave her the first lie of the day. She told me that the complimentary breakfast was warmed and waiting.

I turned toward the lounging area and found Sue already at a table with juice and dried toast. Her back was to me. CNN was dribbling out the latest news. I poured a cup of coffee and walked over to where she sat. I plopped down on the chair opposite her.

"Morning," I said. It seemed the appropriate thing to say, given the circumstances.

Her hands were folded under her chin and she was biting her lower lip. Without moving her head Sue's eyes rose and looked at me. The looked a little red and puffy.

I tried my best to look totally innocent, as if nothing had happened less than ten hours ago. Not that I was keeping track, or anything like that.

The innocent look appeared to work.

"Morning," she said. There was a pregnant pause. "About last night . . ." She didn't finish.

I waited, keeping the look of naiveté, even adding a bit of whimsy to my gaze. I figured I had her fooled.

Sue smiled. "You really look stupid when you stare like that."

Then I smiled, "Guilty as charged, ma'am."

"If I overstepped a boundary last night, Rick, I need to know, because I feel terrible."

"You didn't overstep anything," I said. "You're honest and

open and direct. You were being who you are. Don't feel terrible about that. I haven't been as honest with you, I guess. I don't know what else to say except that we're good. It's okay."

I held the Styrofoam coffee cup in both hands. I could have crushed it to smithereens. To say I was a little tense was an understatement. This was my second lie of the day. I smiled an unconvincing smile. Sue looked at me. Through me, actually. I knew she was smart, and I started to sweat.

"It's six-thirty," she said. "Don't we have to be on the road?" she said.

"Right, partner . . . let's go."

The sawmill was just opening when we took our place for viewing the comings and goings of daily traffic. The road running past was busy with industrial noises: cement trucks off to some project, garbage haulers heading to the local landfill, mill trucks arriving and leaving and other laboring vehicles going their own way on this new day. Greenwood was an aggressive and growing community. The day was also another Mississippi scorcher. We had hoped Jones would arrive within the hour, and, true to form, he and Charlie drove in at 8:00. They repeated their movements of the day before, but this time they had company following them as they exited the mill with the day's load of lumber—us.

Thankful to start the car and run the air, we fell in behind Jones, keeping a car or two between him and us. He drove south to Highway 82 and turned east.

THIRTY-SEVEN

We followed Jones on 82, past Interstate 55, past Winona and on toward Starkville. The drive was made long by the load of timber Jones' truck was hauling, but at last we were nearing Starkville, home of Mississippi State University and about 25,000 happy students, all of whom needed affordable housing. The truck pulled into a residential development and we stopped just before entering. A sign designated this development as the Cheever Addition with 1000 units and surnamed Cheever Construction Company.

Well, little old Cheever Lumber Mill divested itself nicely and was practically self-sufficient. There were obviously subcontractors in this schematic, but Cheever was obviously making a mint in the college-based building market. This was a busy place. Hard-hatted supervisors were examining condos at their various stages of completion. There were many crews of workers, mostly of Mexican persuasion, involved at different levels of construction: one crew working on foundation, another working on superstructure, still another working with electrical and plumbing, another putting on a roof and yet another working inside, painting and finishing. Some condos were completed and FOR SALE signs decorated front lawns. Some were obviously already inhabited.

Cars were parked along the front curbs of some whose parking lots in the rear of the buildings were still being poured with concrete in anticipation of future traffic. There was a significant pool area/cabana central to the complex.

It was a well-organized machine. We could hear the accordion play of Spanish music coming from some radio in the distant fog of dusty wind-blown dirt amid construction equipment and working men and women. We could still see the truck up ahead. Jones had stopped at a site. His load was promptly removed as if on cue by ten or so workers, and he and Charlie worked the ties that had held the freshly cured lumber on board, preparing to return to Greenwood once unloaded. It would be a three quarter's day work for those two, in both the drive to and from Starkville.

Jones and Goode were on the road again in less than an hour, returning the way they had come. Sue and I stayed back a discretionary distance until, as we neared Winona, the truck slowed well before coming to the city limits, blinkered right and turned onto an oil highway called Hollow Road.

I looked at Sue and said, "Looks like our boys are taking a side trip."

"What did you say earlier about Winona?" she asked.

"That there was a general meeting place for FTNF and it was near Winona. Hold on to your bonnet, Miss Richy. We're going for a ride."

We turned behind the truck but slowed to keep a reasonably safe distance between him and us. The road was narrow, tree-lined and wound in a northerly direction, curving here and there. Homes—shacks, rather—dotted the sides of the road. These were nothing more than small sixteen-by-thirty-foot wooden shells. The roofs were more porous than protective, patchwork waxed curtains hung over open, glassless windows, foundations were open underneath, with makeshift porches holding a chair or two and four or five steps rising up to these porches. Most sat on stilts . . . Mississippi poverty at its worst.

We passed a Baptist church with a woodened staked sign at the entrance, the pastor of record crudely painted on a two-by-three-foot piece of plywood nailed to the stake. The pastor of record these days was Jimmy Washington.

We rolled down our windows and kept following Jones. He obviously had no clue of our presence. For five miles we wound around on Hollow Road. When the way opened up for a bit to a cotton field we could see the rig clearly, and we had to slow down quickly to avoid being seen ourselves. But then trees closed about us again. Finally the truck slowed. We slowed too, being about one-eighth of a mile behind, grateful for the trees and curves to hide us from plain sight. The truck disappeared from our full view when it turned off onto a side road. We sped up a little until we saw the road. It was little more than a worn dirt pathway, ungraded and rough. Jones' rig was easy to follow as it both kicked up what dust there was and the empty trailer made noise enough bouncing over the uneven terrain.

In less than a minute the truck sounds on the road ahead became still, and I stopped. Leaving the car doors slightly open to maintain silence, Sue and I moved to a place where we could see without being seen, behind scrub brush just off the road in a stand of trees.

We heard the truck's doors slam shut before we saw them. Jones had parked in a clearing fifty yards from us. The clearing was about an acre in size and in that clearing was an old two-storied barn that had at one time been painted red and had probably held cotton ginned bales. It had obviously been unused for many years. The two went to the front panels and moved the sliding entrance door to the side. It rolled easily and they walked inside.

I whispered to Sue, "I think this could be the place. I don't know if anyone else is coming. We'd better stay close to the car in case we need a quick exit."

"Okay," she said and slid behind me and to my left, so she could also see the barn.

After ten minutes of no action, I turned to suggest to Sue that we leave and come back at a time when no one was there and investigate, as we had at Jones' home. We also had to be out of there before anyone discovered us and ruined the surprise, but what was the surprise? I didn't have a clue. As I turned, I felt a stinging sensation on my ankle, just above the sock line. I looked down to discover I'd been standing close to a fire ant hill. The little shits had found me either appetizing or offensive or both. Either way, about a hundred of them were getting serious with my right shoe and ankle. I let out a short yelp, backed up and swatted at my ankle. They were fighters and biters. I hopped on one leg and lost my balance, falling backward hard on the ground. The stinging hurt and their venom had already caused my ankle to spot red and swell.

Sue thought I'd lost it until she saw the cause. She ran to me and pulled off my shoe and sock, brushing away the last of the little buggers. I sat there on the ground looking up at her, and then looked over to the sand mound that housed the colony. Millions of fire ants were scurrying to defend themselves and their camp.

Sue said, "We have those in Alabama. They can kill you if the stings are numerous and go untreated, and if you're allergic, it can go fast. Your throat just swells up and you can't breathe. I had a girlfriend who was allergic. She had to watch her every move when outside." She looked very concerned. "Are you allergic?"

"I don't think so. It just hurts like hell, and it's starting to itch."

"Well, don't scratch. That'll only make it worse. We'd better get some antiseptic on that ankle right away."

I looked back at the barn. My pained cries hadn't carried to the ears of the men. We would come back.

We slipped back into the car. It started quietly and we drove back to the highway.

In Winoma we stopped at a Walgreen's for some hydrocortisone. Sue ran in to the store and was back to the car in a minute. She rubbed the cream on my foot and ankle. Some of the little flesh eaters had even reached the calf. Zealous little insects they were. Soon the itching stopped, the pain subsided, but the experience taught a valuable lesson: The only good fire ant is a dead one.

"Thanks Sue. I'll be more careful the next time we go traipsing off into the jungles."

"And don't even go near the water," she said.

"Why?"

"Snakes . . . black snakes . . . dangerous snakes."

"Sheesh," I said.

It was two o'clock on a humid afternoon and we hadn't eaten since early morning. So we stopped at a McDonalds off of Highway 82. On entering the restaurant the cool air hit us like a brick wall. One thing I did notice in Mississippi was the air conditioning. All places used it and used it to the optimum potential. It may not have been forty degrees in this McDonalds, but it felt like it.

We went up to the short end of the L-shaped counter and a young black man came to our service. He was the assistant manager, maybe twenty-two years old and courteous. Our order was filled. We sat close to the main entrance, behind the refuse containers. Sue sat with her back to the window and I sat with my back to the serving counter. I had my Twins cap on for sunblock purposes but took it off and laid it on the empty chair beside me while we ate. Sue was digging into a salad and I was digging into extra large fries and a nine-piece chicken special with honey mustard sauce. A Coke sat close by. The restaurant was not particularly crowded at this time of day. I looked over my shoulder and saw maybe three other tables in use.

This McDonalds was an older model with an open floor plan. I did note that in the far corner an elderly black woman stood looking over the dining area. Apparently she was an employee who cleaned tables after use. I smiled at her, but she returned a noncommittal look. I turned my vigor to the chicken. Sue had bottled water on ice in a paper cup. I was about to say something to get a rise out of her when I looked out to the parking lot.

While my attention had been averted by the food, Sam Jones and Charlie Goode had pulled into the truckers' parking lot and were coming in. There was no place for us to hide.

THIRTY-EIGHT

"Sue, we've got company."

She turned her head.

"No, don't look. A couple of friends decided to share our fine taste in cuisine. Look inconspicuous."

At that word the door opened and in walked Sam and Charlie.

We were on their right as they entered but we were hidden by the trash containers. They turned and took a right, directly behind me toward the restrooms which were twenty feet past our table.

Sue looked at me in surprise. "Well, what about that?"

"They don't know us and I don't want to be in any position that would get their attention. Maybe they're not here to eat. Maybe they're here just to use the facilities. Keep a low profile, here they come."

Out the restroom door they came and to the short side of the counter directly behind me. Sam Jones, the man I wanted to bring down along with his FTNF buddies, was right here. If he'd known that, he wouldn't have been so at ease. Shit, I could have reached out my left arm and touched him, but Sue and I both kept our faces to task. Sue kept one hand to her forehead, shading her face. The problem—what if they ordered and sat next to us? Our faces would no longer be an unknown, and then plan B would have to go into affect. Of course I had no plan B. But, as it appeared by what happened next, Sam was not here to eat.

The black assistant manager came over to take Jones' order.

"Y'all ain't got no paper towels in yer restroom," Jones said in arrogant bluster.

"Yes sir," the young man replied. "We have automatic warm

air blowers for your use."

"Wal see, boy, I been travlin' all day and I gotta wipe my ass. I need paper towels to wipe my ass and y'all ain't got no paper towels. Wha' you gonna do about that, boy?"

Did I hear what I thought I'd just heard? Jones wasn't talking in a soft voice. He wanted the whole restaurant to hear what he was saying.

The manager, a white woman, heard the words and was over behind her assistant but stayed out of it. However, she was definitely there to observe.

And Jones, having liked what he said so much, said it again.

"Ah need paper towels to wipe my ass, boy, and y'all ain't got no paper towels. Now, ah need tah have my ass wiped! Wha' you gonna do about that, boy?"

Sue was looking at me. She must have seen my muscles tense themselves to pounce position because she put her hands over mine. I looked at her and she moved her head slightly side to side.

The black assistant manager kept his cool and said, "I'm very sorry, sir, but we don't have paper towels in our restrooms. We changed over to warm air dryers a while ago. I'm sorry."

Jones said, "Wahl then I'll jest have tah go someplace else and eat mah meal and wipe mah ass." And with that Jones and his silent but smiling friend made their way out, swaggering the whole way.

I watched them go to their truck, pull out onto 82 and head toward Greenwood. I was huffing and puffing and said in a not so quiet whisper, "I could have told that ass-wipe where to go to do his business."

"Shhh! It's over Rick," said Sue.

In the meantime, back inside, things behind the counter went about as before. The assistant manager had seemed to pass the test of customer dissatisfaction with his manager, because they were talking earnestly behind the counter and the young man was smiling. At the same time the black lady who was cleaning tables had come over to empty the trash bins next to Sue and me.

When I saw that she was within speaking distance, I leaned toward her and said, "How can some people be as stupid as that man?"

She didn't say a word, but threw us a courtesy smile and walked away.

I looked at Sue. "She must have heard all that. That woman should be mad as hell at those racist comments. 'How am I gonna wipe my ass, *boy*? What are ya gonna do about that, *boy*?' My God, he verbally and racially attacked that young man. Why didn't that woman react? Maybe she's deaf."

"Rick, I see that you have much to learn about the South. That woman didn't acknowledge us, not because she's deaf, but more than likely she didn't react to us because we are white.

"The stigma continues, especially in Mississippi. Blacks have not historically had a conversational love affair with whites down here. There is a huge lack of trust. For her to acknowledge a white man's criticism against another white man and for you to expect her consensual agreement, well, that would put her in a position of being critical toward a white. She wouldn't dare do that. Know why? Because *you* might just be baiting her to a position that would give you every right to come down hard on her for being an uppity nigger."

"But we're not that way."

"No, we're not, but she doesn't know that. She just doesn't dare carry on a conversation with you about the racist actions of another white man. To her, you're just another white man."

"Jesus Christ. How do we bridge that gap?"

"I don't know, Rick. I just don't know."

Our meal was technically finished when Jones had first started his diatribe. We went to use the restrooms before we left. I noted that the air dryers worked fine. I should have kicked the shit out of Jones! I walked out before Sue and went to move our food trays to the trash. What I found was that our trays had already been removed and my cap, which had been lying on the seat beside me, had been placed very carefully on the table top in front of where I had been sitting. I looked across the dining area. The black lady was standing attentively at the far corner. She sent a quiet smile my way, a smile of affirmation, crossing the gap of black/white, beyond fear, nodding her head a fraction that only I could see.

Sue came out. "Thanks for cleaning off the table. Are you ready?"

"I am now."

THIRTY-NINE

"Those two need direction in their lives, that's all," said Sue after we got back in the car.

"Yah, and I'll be their direction finder," I said.

"Jones is too far gone at his age," she said.

"And I think the kid's nature has pretty much implanted itself in his ego. The only change in direction for Charlie would probably include some hard time at a correctional institution. I think Josh was that way."

"What now?"

"Back to the barn."

I had turned the car back to Hollow Road and to the barn, parking a respectable distance off the road. From there we could make a quick exit if necessary.

The barn looked empty and we went directly to the sliding doors. They weren't locked, though there was a padlock and chain inserted through the handles and the lock appeared to be closed in position. It was made to look locked.

"Apparently not everyone has a key," Sue said.

"Or something is going to happen here pretty soon," I said.

With that thought, we went inside, closing the door behind us.

The interior was dimly lit by sunlight seeping through open cracks in the boarded siding, giving the impression of barred shadows on the opposing walls. Dust particles floated in and out between the sun and shadow. The area covered about forty-by-forty-foot square and looked to be about twenty feet high; the floor was hardened dirt. We walked and observed. Opposite from the entrance, a crude ladder was nailed to the outside wall studs. The ladder was mounted to a lofted area where an opening had been cut in the back center of the loft. The entire loft covered about half the space of the barn and was probably used as an overflow for cotton bales. Its floor was about twelve feet above the ground.

At this same end of the barn and in the center, a makeshift podium with three fruit crates stacked one on another faced the front. I walked over to the crates, and noticed out of the corner of my eye what appeared to be an interior closet at the far corner of the barn. I went to its door; it opened to a six by ten foot storage area. It was empty.

"Is there anything in there?" asked Sue. Her voice echoed loudly inside the barn.

"No," I whispered, putting my finger to my lips.

"Sorry," she said.

Sue was standing behind the stacked crates. She faced the open end of the barn as if she were about to address a classroom of students. The top crate was sitting on its side with the open end facing her. She bent down slightly and reached her hand inside, pulling out a paper notebook. She set it on top of the crate.

"Rick, come here," Sue whispered, motioning me over with her right hand.

The notebook was college-ruled, similar to the one we'd found in Jones' house. The pages were all blank except for the first; on the top middle of it were the words, "Task to be completed," and scratched on its top right side margin was the calendar date, June 30. That was today's date.

I turned to Sue. "It looks like we might be busy. Maybe the whole gang will be here. If so, they'll have two extra guests they hadn't counted on."

Sue looked at the notebook, then at me, and gave a "thumbs up."

That was when I hesitated, realizing that this was a serious step and that I was about to put Sue in harm's way.

She sensed it immediately.

"Rick! Don't go there. I'm here for the long haul."

I looked at Sue, her face in shadows, her hair uncombed and wet from the humidity of the middle afternoon, locks clinging to her face, which was dirty from the combination of wind and humidity and dust, and something happened. I don't know how or why it happened, there in an old barn in the middle of Mississippi on a sweltering hot afternoon, but life just became more complicated because of this woman, and I lost focus.

"Rick? Talk to me," Sue reached over and shook my arm. "Hello. Earth to Rick."

"Um," I said, coming back to some sense of reality. "I'm thinking about a plan here, an actual plan. Uh, do we want to be on the outside looking in or on the inside looking in?"

"What?"

"We could hide in the loft and be really close to the action, but it leaves no escape in case of emergency. Or we could stay outside and try to hear what's happening inside, with an escape route if needed."

"There are two of us," Sue said. "We could cover both ends of that question."

"You mean one out and one in," I said.

"Sure."

"I don't think I like that idea. Let's take a look up in the loft and see what we have there."

I went over to the wall and reached up, gripped a wooden rung two feet above my head and pulled. It resisted my weight. Then I stepped onto the first board, which was a foot above the floor, and set my body weight there. It held me easily. I started the climb up. The rungs were about a foot and a half apart, and I disappeared into the square opening above, lifting myself up through the opening and onto the loft floor. I reached out and stepped forward. It was darker up here than down below and I had to give my eyes time to adjust. A flashlight would help. I made a mental note of that. The loft was empty. It had not been used for a long while. The floor was filthy. As I walked, whiffs of grime settled between the floorboards and fell down below. That was not good. If someone were to position themselves up here, they should first sweep an area free of loose dirt.

I stepped back down and said, "It's strong enough to hold me. No one's been up there for years. The floor shows no sign of use. There's a layer of dirt we have to deal with, but no human footprints. Only birds and rodents have used that loft lately. I'm going to hide up there. You stay outside in a safe place close to car and road. If there looks like trouble, you get out to safety."

"That doesn't sound like a very good plan to me," she said.

"I never promised you a rose garden," I said.

"Beg your pardon?"

I hopped the last step and faced Sue. "No arguments," I said.

"I don't like it and I don't care whether or not you want an argument. You have one."

"Now look here." I stood toe-to-toe with her. "You need to be reminded who's the boss. This is my cross to bear and you came along to support. This is the time I need support, not debate. Either you will go along with this or I do it myself and you go home."

"Simple as that, huh?"

"No, it's not simple and it's not easy. But nevertheless this is the way it will be."

"Okay, okay, Mr. Hoity-Toity. I am the support."

"Thank you," I replied. "We can discuss the merits of this when it's over."

"Oh you can be certain of that," she said.

"What time is it?" I asked. "I left my watch back at the motel."

Sue looked at hers. "It's four-thirty."

"I don't want to risk going back to Greenwood. I just don't know what time the action might start here in the barn. Jones left the entrance unlocked. I think that means that others will be coming sooner rather than later because they need access to the barn for whatever reason. I want the car hidden well. I think your idea about one of us outside and the other inside is a good idea. I want you placed where you can see the goings and comings and still be well protected from searching eyes, and I want me settled in the loft. Let's get some food and hydration right now. It may be a long night. Oh, and speaking of night, let's stop back at Walgreens and buy two small flashlights just, in case."

We drove back to Winona and McDonalds. There'd been a shift change and this afternoon's excitement was ancient history to the new workers. Sue and I had chicken and water with three waters each "to go." It was a short break, but refreshing.

Walgreens was as good as its name. There were all styles of artificial torches for sale. On the way to the counter to make the purchase, I passed the electronic aisle and my eye caught some mini-recorders on a shelf. I picked up a digital voice-activated recorder and batteries. We paid at the front and went back to the car.

Back on Hollow Road, we looked for a hiding place for the Chevy and found a nearly level ditch a hundred yards past the barn. I drove into the ditch and on into the woods where there was opening enough for the car. I turned the car in among the trees and faced Hollow Road. In case of a quick retreat, all we had to do was hop in, start it up and drive straight out. The car was slightly visible from the road, so we found brush and fallen limbs of trees, accumulated through the years of storms and winds and old age, and placed enough on and around the car to hide it from plain view.

Deciding to stay to the trees, we worked our way back to the barn, angling our direction toward where we thought the barn stood. It took five minutes to find the opening around the barn. I saw that no one was about so I began looking for a place for Sue to hide.

Before I'd walked forty paces I heard Sue exclaim, "Rick!"

I turned, but she wasn't there.

"Rick!" she cried out again.

I followed her voice. It seemed to be coming from an old, fully-leafed Sawtooth oak tree standing at the edge of the yard. I walked over to the oak, which stood about thirty feet high, and looked up.

I heard her say, "Hi."

I still couldn't see her, but she was certainly 'up a tree.' Finally, Sue moved her legs and I saw her. She was twenty feet up, nestled in the crotch of two branches that extended outward from the main trunk. If it was deer season, Sue couldn't have been better protected from sight.

"How did you get up there?" I asked. The first weight-bearing limb of the tree was a good nine feet from the ground.

"Apparently, I'm still in pretty good shape, Mr. Burns," she said, slipping into sarcasm mode.

"You are absolutely invisible from down here. How's the view of the barn entrance?"

"It's clear when I move one small limb with my hand."

"Do you have water?"

"I'm good," she said.

"Are you comfortable enough?"

"As comfy as a hibernating bear with a belly full of food."

"God, that's weak."

"Hanging out a bit too much with literaries, I guess."

"Right . . ."

Then she was somber. "Rick, be careful. I wouldn't want anything to happen to you."

"Kind of hard to be serious with a girl in a tree. I'll see you when this place clears out."

I walked over to the barn entrance. We'd closed the doors just as Jones had left them earlier, and I went inside, over to the ladder and up into the loft.

I found what would be the most comfortable and inconspicuous area of the attic. I cleaned out the dirt accumulation without raising too much dust and lay down. There was a relatively large open knothole in the wood which gave me a view of the goings-on below. With minimal movement, I could see the whole of the barn, including the entrance. Too much movement, though, and they'd see my head and the show would be over.

So, now the waiting began. I'd left Sue in the tree nearly an hour earlier. I figured it must be getting close to the time a meeting might be held, giving the members time to get home from their workday, eat, and drive here to join hands, rejoicing in their hate-filled hobby.

And I was right.

FORTY

At first it was only the idea of a sound I thought I heard, but then it became distinct. A vehicle was making its way off Hollow Road onto the pathway to the barn. It sounded like a truck.

It slowed at the barn entry, circled away from the doorway and the sound of reverse came to my ears. The truck backed up to the entrance. I heard two doors open and close.

The barn door slid open and sunlight streamed in. I knew Sue could see the new arrivals, but I could see only silhouettes in the sunlight that streamed through the opening... two men, by their voices. They joked about the weather. Then I heard a scraping noise. They were obviously taking a weighted object from the truck and were carrying it into the barn. Then I could see them: two men in jeans and work boots, probably in their twenties, each lugging either side of what appeared to be a gasoline-powered electric generator.

This answered any questions about holding nighttime meetings. The generator was set down close to the entrance and the men went back outside. They returned, bringing in electric cords and two tripod stands holding industrial halogen work lights, the kind used for large outdoor night projects.

They tried starting the generator. The electric starter kicked on. The generator ran roughly at first and then died. One of the men swore, adjusted the choke, tried again and the machine caught and began to purr smoothly. They switched on the lights. There was real candle power in those bulbs, enough to light the interior of the barn. The brilliance was such that I felt naked and exposed in the loft, and was thankful for the floorboards beneath me.

The two set up the lights at angles pointing toward and

crisscrossing beams in front of the podium, thus illuminating the walls behind and to either side of it. I moved my head away from the opening for a bit. Then I looked back below. The two had left the barn again, but I heard them rummaging in the truck outside. In they came once again, this time each carrying what appeared to be sturdy rolled paper. It looked like posterboard.

And indeed, that's what it was. There were six posters. They unrolled each and tacked them onto the podium and sides of the barn where the light would shine most directly. I watched in silent revulsion at what I saw.

On the front of the podium the organization's name, FTNF, was printed in six-inch red letters, running vertically from top to bottom. In one-inch red lettering, shooting off from the large letters, was the spelling of the rest, Finished Tasks Need Finishing, all on a black background, small tears of blood dripping from each "i."

But this was expected. I would have been disappointed without that. What sent my stomach into emotional overdrive were the large posters tacked on to the walls of the barn where the halogen lights threw their terrible beams.

Directly behind the podium was a four-by-six foot Stars and Bars with the words, "We shall rise again" at the bottom. The two posters on either side of this symbol were what made me truly ill.

On these three-by-five foot posters were the photographed faces of Abraham Lincoln, John F. Kennedy, Martin Luther King, Jr., and Bobby Kennedy. Four men who championed civil rights for human beings, assassinated by cowards with guns who gave these men no fighting chance at defense. Across each face, drawn in blood-red paint was a diagonal line. And here was the group of cowards who glorified in it all. It sickened me.

I heard other vehicles driving up to the barn. It was dusk outside, but bright as day in here. Sue would be watching it all unfold from her vantage point but she wouldn't know what was happening inside. I knew she was safe but I feared for what these men were capable of doing. They were serious about what it was they believed, and that would carry over to physical injury to more than just church buildings. It already had in Colorado.

Men were arriving and saluting one another, not in a military way, but in a joyful playful manner that suggested intelligences just dangerous enough to do injury to innocents. I held my breath when I saw Sam Jones walk in, with Charlie by his side. Jones was wearing jeans like the others and working boots. It was like a uniform with these guys. He had on a plain black tee-shirt but in addition to that, Jones wore a shoulder holster with a gun.

The crowd of men gathered, greeting him with vigorous hand stabbings in the air and the stomping of feet on the dirt floor. Jones acknowledged them as he walked to the front. The rest gathered round, even Charlie, leaving a cleared area of about 10 feet between them and Jones, a respectful distance, it appeared.

I had the digital recorder in my right hand, and pushed the voice activator.

Jones said, "Y'all are here tah prepare for the next step for FTNF. Several weeks ago we lost two brothers who fought for the cause. Terry Sims is dead, y'all know that. But who was the otha who fought for the cause and died? It was a brother who joined us. He found a friend in me and acted on the cause. He finished a task for the cause. His name was Holston. He lived over in Ruleville but moved tah Colorada a while back. He and me talked about the future and this Holston fella, well, he went out and eliminated a niggah and white bitch couple."

Cheers from below. My stomach turned over on itself. He was just warming up.

"Now y'all know that this is what it's all about anyway," Jones continued. "This Holston boy eliminated them, but now he's dead. He got arrested, an he died in jail. They say it was a accident. We know there ain't no such thing as a accident in jail, don't we, men?"

At this a negative booing went up from the crowd, and I tried to get a count of men during this raucous noise. They numbered, for all I could see in the glare of the lights, probably twenty-five to thirty.

Jones went on, "Now we are gonna honor that young man's sacrifice with a elimination ourselves. We have burned the niggah churches. Now we is gonna burn some niggahs!"

Loud cheers.

"Tomorraw night there's a Baptist church meetin' over in Holmes County. All the niggah leaders will be there tah discuss their burned churches. Shit, they is gonna be suprized when they find themselves burnin' in their own fuckin' church."

"How we gonna do that?" came a voice from the pack.

"Well, I'll tell yah hows we gonna do that," said Jones. "The meetin' is scheduled for tomorraw night. Charlie and me got enough fertilizer and fuel tah burn a hundred churches. Charlie and me'll bring all the shit we need. All y'all bring yer guns. When it looks like tha niggah meetin' is on full speed, we surround the church and start a little party of our own.

"Charlie and me already staked out the church. We gonna meet at Bhonson's Corner outside a Lexington. Y'all know where that is. We go togetha from there. All y'all will follow me and Charlie. We'll give the orders from there. There'll be one man at ev'ry other winda and at ev'ry door. That'll be plenty enough tah git it goin'. It's gonna be hot and when the niggahs run out, and that's when we all will have some target practice. It's time we showed 'em all that their civil rights don't mean a thing here in Mississippi."

Cheers.

"They think they's equal to whites. Fuck no! You know what, boys? We gonna show the pimp Uncle Tom government of this here USA that times are a changin'! The South shall rise again! Finished tasks need finishin'!"

More hoots and hollers and clapping and fist-thrusts.

With that Jones walked away from the podium and into the throng of eager believers. They rallied around this miserable excuse for a human being and the garbage that issued from his mouth. And worse than that, it looked strangely like this group of misguided anarchists meant business. If they did, it wasn't even a bit funny.

I rolled over onto my back to catch a full breath. When I did, the floor beneath me creaked slightly, enough to get my attention. I only hoped it hadn't caught the attention of those below. I heard nothing suspicious. The talk among the men carried up to me and my stupid move went unheard. That left me to worry about Sue. She seemed safe where she was, but I imagined her falling out of the tree and into trouble. Certainly she must have wondered what was going on inside and would have questions.

The crowd began to filter away and the posters were taken down, the podium dismantled. But what were they going to do with the crates? Probably take them with them to remove all evidence of having been here.

Then I heard the very clear voices of several men walking toward the ladder for the loft.

FORTY-ONE

"Let's put these crates up here," someone said, and he began to climb the first two steps. A beam from a flashlight broke through the curtain of shadows that hid me from casual view. The shaft of light was a clumsy circle targeting the roof of the loft as the man stepped up to what would be a discovery he'd not counted on. I thought quickly. In survival mode, I tensed and rose to a partial three-point stance, knuckles on the floor, weight slightly forward, and toes on end. Whatever happened, it would be quickly. If I had any advantage it was of surprise, but that would give me only so much time. There was no plan B. My heart took a jump. I was poised.

"Nah, it's easier to just keep this shit in the storage room over in the corner. It'll be easier to get at next time."

"Okay Horace. Y'all are so fuckin' smart and know all the answers." The voice was too close for comfort.

"Shit, yes. That's 'cause I'm yer older brother," said the other.

That was a pant wetter. The young man stepped back down to the ground and I heard the crates being put into the closet, the door closed, and then the lights went out, the generator turned off. It was pitch black now. The same flashlight beam again broke through the darkness. The generator and lights were taken away. The sounds of vehicles starting and wheels turning and spinning on the pathway leading out to the main road were all that was left. Soon those sounds faded and it was dead quiet.

I waited and listened. No sounds. Normally one would say it's too quiet, but I welcomed the silence. I reached into my pocket and pulled out a small penlight. The beam helped me find the recorder where I'd placed it next to the knothole. I turned the recorder power off and walked to the ladder and looked down.

Putting the light in my mouth, I directed the beam to the rungs, stretched my right foot and hand out from the loft floor over the open space of the entry hole and grabbed for the supporting two-by-fours to start the climb down. Doing this in relative dark was challenging and I had to feel for the next rung while preparing to let go of the handhold above. It took a little faith, but I felt terra firma under my feet soon enough. I took the penlight from my mouth and started toward the barn door. When I reached the door, I pulled the handle to slide it open, but it wouldn't move. Shit! The door had been padlocked shut from the outside.

I hadn't counted on that.

"Rick?" Sue's voice came from the other side.

"Hey, girl, how are you?" I asked.

"I'm fine. How are *you*?"

"Things are just hunky-dory in the old barn, but it looks like we have a little problem with the door," I said.

"This chain and lock are strong. I can't break it open," she said. "There must be another way out of there."

"I didn't see another door. There are no windows, but wait a minute—I never went inside the small storage room at the back of the barn. There might be a door there."

"I'll meet you there," said Sue.

I turned on the penlight again, made my way to the storage closet and opened the door. The crates were thrown in haphazardly and I kicked one while scanning the area with the light. There it was. The door blended in with the frame of the building, the only difference between it and the walls being that the door had a latch.

Sue was already on the other side, pulling at the door.

"Rick, this is locked, too."

"No problem," I said. It was a simple heavy-duty latch. I pulled down on a metal ring which lifted the steal bar from the interlocked position and the door swung open. I closed it and the latch caught, relocking the door.

It was as dark outside as in, but Sue was there with her flashlight. We walked back to the car in silence; the only sounds were those of Mississippi nights, the hoot owls and field mice. I removed the camouflage from the rental car and slid in behind the steering wheel.

As Sue got into the car on the other side, she asked, "Well, what went on in there? All I could hear were shouts that sounded like cheering. I was worried they'd found you."

She faced me by adjusting her body so her back leaned against the door frame, and she crossed one leg under the other.

"I'll tell you," I said, "but first tell me what happened outside."

"It was quiet outside after everybody went in the barn," she said. "I counted thirty men in all: twenty-eight inside and two who stayed outside. Those two stationed themselves at the road. I think they were the security force. They carried shotguns. I never heard what they were saying to one another, because they spoke in whispers. Other than that it was uneventful, until it was over and everybody left."

I nodded, and then brought out the digital recorder, rewound and pushed "play." What I'd recorded repeated itself in all its ugliness.

Sue sat with open mouth, her eyes focused on the recorder as though it were alive. "Rick, this is far and away too dangerous now," she said when we'd finished listening. "We have to tell the authorities."

"You're right, but look at this scenario. What would happen if two Yanks walked up to the local cops with the kind of story we have to tell? We look like two street bums from another world, and then ask them to listen to a recording such as this? Even I wouldn't believe us. Besides that, how can we be certain the cops are on our side? It's possible some of them were at this meeting. I'll call Jim. He'll make sure we have an attentive audience."

FORTY-TWO

Sue reached into the glove box and retrieved my cell phone. I had full power but there was no signal.

"We need to get within range of a tower," I said.

I started the car and drove back to the main highway where we tried again. This time the signal was full. I pulled over to the side of the road, keyed the Estes Park police office, and Jim answered at the other end.

"What did you get yourselves into down there in Mississippi?" he asked after I'd told him our story. He went on without waiting for an answer. "What's the name of the county seat where this is going down?"

"Sue and I have a road map we've been using. She's looking it up. Just a minute . . ."

Sue said, "It's Lexington, in Holmes County."

"I'll call the Mississippi Bureau of Investigation in Jackson and the sheriff's office in Lexington," Jim said. "Between those two, my word from this end, along with your recording, there'll be quick action. I have your phone number and motel address. You go back there now and wait for a call. How far from there are you now?"

"We're less than an hour away," I said.

"Okay," Jim said. "Get going. And by the way, Rick, this is a dangerous, foolish, wonderful thing you're doing."

The line went dead.

Sue asked, "What did he say?"

"He said that you are the most beautiful girl in Colorado and should know better than to hang with someone like me," I said. I protected my right rib cage with my right arm merely as a defensive measure.

"Well, I know that, stupid." Using the thumb as a launching pad and the middle finger of her left hand, she clicked my head with a quick snap. "But what did he really say, Rick?"

"Ouch." I moved my right hand to my head. That exposed my right rib cage and the jab was thrust. "Ouch. Okay, okay."

I told her what Jim had said as we set off toward Greenwood, more relaxed than we'd been for the last few days. FTNF would be but a wisp of a terrible past. I felt almost relief, and could see that Sue felt the same way. Bob Evermore and Amy Crenshaw would, in some small way, reap a greater justice for what Josh Holston alone did to them. The roots of Holston's hate would be stopped as well. I owed their memory that much.

I looked over to Sue. She'd leaned back against the seat, her face turned to me and she smiled. "We did good, Rick."

"We did good, Sue Richy." With my left hand on the wheel, I inadvertently moved my right hand across the seat toward Sue. She looked down at my hand and at me and took my hand with hers.

We both relaxed, breathed a sigh of relief, and drove in quiet peace to the motel to wait for a call.

FORTY-THREE

The call came at 11:30. Sue and I had showered up. I'd convinced her that bagged chips and candy bars were nutritious snacks as we sat waiting in my room. I turned on the TV. The FOX Network had just declared itself "Fair and Balanced" when I answered the phone, "Rick Burns here."

"Mr. Burns, this is Agent Smithland with the Mississippi Bureau of Investigation. I have been in communication with Sheriff Harris in Colorado. He has filled me in on you and the situation you have encountered. I understand you have a recording we would be interested in listening to. I would like to meet with you in your motel room in half an hour. Is that too soon?"

"I'll be ready. Thanks."

"Mr. Burns, we'll see soon enough who should be thanking whom."

Sue cleaned up the food mess and we arranged the table for the interview that would shortly take place.

I answered the door at his knock. Agent Smithland shook hands with us both, and he seated himself in the proffered chair at the table, I sat on the other side, and Sue sat on the edge of the bed. The recorder sat in the middle of the table, like a witness in a court of law. I guess it was a witness of sorts.

Smithland was of average build, about forty-five years old, with alert eyes that took in the whole room as soon as he entered . . . and he was African American. He wore a pair of jeans and white mock turtleneck under a sport jacket. He removed the jacket before sitting. This uncovered a Glock .45 in a shoulder holster. I have seen these guns in action while working with Jim Harris during summer training sessions with the Estes Park

Police Department. They are very effective at what they do.

"Sorry 'bout the gun," he said. "It comes in handy from time to time." He didn't wait for a response. "Is this the recorder?" he asked, getting right down to business.

"Yes," I said. "It's voice-activated and, well, I'll just let it speak for itself."

"Great," he said. "I may have a question or two after we've listened to it."

The recorder told its story.

At the conclusion Smithland turned to me and said, "This is some serious stuff. I've heard the rhetoric before. I was born and raised in Mississippi, Mr. Burns."

His face looked toward nothing in particular and with a sigh, he continued. "I grew up 'yes sirring' and 'no sirring' to the likes of Jones. I saw my family live in poverty for no other reason than that they were kept down by the likes of people like Jones. I saw whites as superior till I became old enough to understand. Then I directed my own disgust back at the injustice of it all. I became hateful myself. For the sake of education, I'll tell you this. One day my pastor, who thought there may be some hope for someone like me, told me two things that have driven me to where I am today.

"The first: Don't lower yourself to the level of hateful whites. It will only eat you up from the inside out, and besides, they probably don't even know how you feel. And if they did, they wouldn't care.

"And the second: The best thing you can make out of your enemy is a friend.

"Those two bits of wisdom helped me survive. I vowed to find a way to rid the world of hateful prejudice. Part of my reason for getting into law enforcement was to help nail these misguided human beings. We can't get them for the rhetoric alone, but we can end their campaign of terror by catching them in the act. The more terrible the act, the longer we can put them away. Now, I have a few questions for you."

"Shoot," I said. I looked at his gun. "Sorry, maybe the wrong word."

"No mind," he said. "We have to work quickly. I need to take this recorder to Jackson. It is now evidence."

"Sure." What was I going to do? Wrestle him for it?

He continued, "The two of you have been a blessing to us. But your job is done. And I thank you, but what happens from now till the conclusion will be strictly law enforcement. It'll be dangerous and you have to stay put. We'll get in touch when it's over."

"We wouldn't intrude on this," I said. "But I have a question for you."

"Shoot," he said, and added, "We talk that way too."

"Yes, well, how do you catch them in the act? How far do you let it go?"

"For your ears only, because you have worked so hard—we've already started. You see, Jim Harris is respected in every agency of law enforcement. He paid his dues. His word to us was enough to form and act on a plan. My listening to the tape only reinforced what it is we'll do.

"The church is being watched. Its pastor has been notified that the meeting he planned for—" he looked at his watch "—for tonight, is off. Other 'pastors' will be there. Those pastors will be carrying fire and brimstone of a different sort. And they will have many friends hidden outside. Those friends will be me and thirty of my closest comrades. The flames will begin but we'll have the stuff there to extinguish any fire. And what do we get? Attempted Murder One for the fire-starters, including charges of terrorism and civil rights hate crimes. Their actions will reward those gutless wonders with seventy years in Parchman. The old phrase 'Mississippi justice,' as they like to put it, works both ways. They're all equally guilty, and real Mississippi justice will take them down. If they start shooting? Lord help them then."

Smithland rose with the recorder in hand and went to the door, turning as he opened it. "Thanks again, Mr. Burns, Miss Richy."

I closed the door. Sue and I looked at one another.

"Thank you, Mr. Burns," she said with formality.

"Thank you, Miss Richy," I replied with sarcasm. "I'm not settling for a stay-at-home posture with this," I added.

"Rick, you said you wouldn't intrude."

"But I didn't say I would stay here either. Let's get some sleep on this and talk about it in the morning over breakfast. It's late, and I'm beat. And you don't look so good yourself."

"Thanks . . . just what a girl likes to hear," she said. "I'll see you at breakfast then."

"G'night," I said.

Sue walked to the door. Then she turned and walked back to me, kissed me on my left cheek, feathery light, like a sister, smiled a "Good night yourself," smile, and left the room.

It felt right.

FORTY-FOUR

I hit the pillow thinking about Bob Evermore and Amy Crenshaw. I would see Sam Jones and company get theirs the next night. Agent Smithland had the look of a man who had lived through the hate of prejudice and overcome the plight he might otherwise have fallen into, hateful himself toward whites he once conceived were his enemy. He'd do the job, and I would stay out of his way, but I wouldn't be denied a part in it, either.

But sleep didn't come. I opened up the Dell and logged on to the hotel wi-fi. There were some things I needed to check, including e-mail from home. Steve wanted to know what was happening. I wrote enough to satisfy his curiosity and clicked "send."

After reading through news stories, checking my bank account, and searching for more info on FTNF (with no results), I was getting drowsy and closed shop. Then I lay back down, closed my eyes, my mind wandered, and I thought about a kiss.

The ringing phone woke me from a deep sleep. I turned over and looked at the clock as I picked up the receiver. It was 8:30.

"Huh?" I said groggily.

"Am I eating by myself this morning?" asked Sue.

"I'll be right down."

Ten minutes later, with laptop in hand, I slopped my way into the lounge and to breakfast, poured a cup of coffee and grabbed a powdered sugar-covered donut. Sue was sitting with the *Clarion-Ledger* folded in front of her, CNN working its magic on the flat screen in the background.

"Anything interesting?" I asked, sitting down beside her.

"No," she said. "The world wags on, but the Peanuts gang stays forever young in the comic section. I sometimes forget that

Charles Schulz is not with us anymore."

I sipped the hot coffee and swore when it burned my upper lip. The powdered sugar melted in my mouth. I stole a drink from Sue's water glass.

"Did Charlie Brown ever get the red-headed girl?" I asked.

"I don't believe he ever had the nerve to even speak to her. He loved her from a distance," Sue said. "The red-headed girl will be forever a symbol of unrequited love."

"Charlie was a fool," I said.

"He wasn't the only man in that category."

I pretended not to hear. Sue just stared. I looked back, giving my best dumb and dumber mug.

"*Wha-a-a-t?*" I whined.

Sue smirked a "you're so hopeless" look, changed gears and asked, "What are we going to do?"

Thankful for this reprieve, I folded my arms and examined the last bits of powered sugar on the plate, pushed it away and said, "I logged on to Google Earth last night and got an aerial view of the Lexington environs. Let me show you."

I opened the Dell and logged on, showing Sue what I found last night and pointing to the screen.

"I figured that a safe place for us would be to stay near Route 12 leading northwest out of Lexington," I told her. "Bhonson's Corner is a deserted gas station on Old Tchula Road off Route 12."

"How did you know that?" she asked.

"I learned a long time ago, when you are in strange country and need directions, besides the local gas station, go to the town library. They'll know where to find things because they've got the resources to use if all else fails. I found that a library plat map was very helpful once when looking for an ancient geographical landmark out in Utah. Plus, the aged librarian knew exactly what I was looking for. She even offered to drive me there."

"What were you looking for?" Sue asked.

"Some things must remain a secret," I replied. "Anyway, I called the city library before coming down and asked about Bhonson's Corner. The answer was swift and direct." I pointed at the screen again. "Here is what appears to be a roadside parking area right off Route 12, just east of the Old Tchula Road. We could park there, far enough away to be unobtrusive yet close enough to witness anything coming from the direction of the church. It's right here, two minutes off 12 on Ferguson Road, which lies just east of the rest area."

"Computers amaze me," she said. "When do we go?"

I closed the laptop. "I think we should get there early enough to look like we belong there. It's quite wooded around this area. We can take a picnic along and pretend we're travelers stopping to enjoy the scenery. By the way, what's the day like?" I asked.

"Oh, it's much cooler than yesterday. It rained earlier this morning... while you were sleeping." She was taunting me. "So, the humidity is ninety-nine percent but the temperature should get no higher than eighty-nine degrees."

"Good," I said. "Then let's get going and find a picnic store."

"A picnic store? What, pray God, is a picnic store?"

"It's a Northern thing. You Southerners wouldn't understand."

"I lived in North Birmingham and I never heard of it."

"Give me a break," I said. "Can you say Walmart?"

"That's better, Mr. Smarty-pants."

"It's going to be a long day," I said. "And a short night, God willing."

We went back to our rooms and got ready for the day ahead. I put on jeans and my CU Buffs tee. The car was filled with gas and Walmart supplied us with picnic items for the duration: a cooler with bagged ice and sodas, tea, water, lunch meats, bread and butter, pickles and mayo, a hot radish mustard for my tastes, plus chips, cookies and trail mix bars. We weren't going to starve.

It was noon when we started out on South Highway 49 for the forty-five minute drive to Lexington. At the junction of 49 and 12 we turned left, passing both Old Tchula Road and the picnic area which did indeed include tables and trees, and on to Ferguson Road where we made a U-turn.

"The church is a mile south from here," I said. "We'd better stay away for now, I suppose."

"I agree," said Sue.

The sun beat down as we drove the short way back to the

picnic ground. The area it occupied was about two acres and had a mini dirt road system that wound its way around and about the trees and tables. A few of the tables had in-ground grills adjacent for cooking. There was a central water pipe rising out of the ground with a spigot, and there were two privies set off in the back center of the park. Several large metal waste cans were strategically placed to discourage littering. We found the shade of a maple that protected us both from the heat and from full vision of passing traffic.

Sue and I got out and stretched our legs a bit. I decided that moving a picnic table, which otherwise sat in open view, back toward our car would give us ample protection from curious eyes. Sue helped me lift and carry the table back to our site and we placed it under the same maple tree. From this vantage point we could see traffic move along the highway, and if we walked close to the highway we could even see the junction at Ferguson Road which was about a football field away.

I opened a Coke and a cranberry almond trail mix bar and sat behind the wheel of the car, which kicked out dry cool air, and enjoyed my private picnic. Sue, on the other hand, was outside walking the dirt road around the park area. She was in shape; I gave her credit for that. What I hadn't given her enough credit for was her strength of character and sense of humor. In addition, given her physical strength, this woman would live well in to her hundreds. Pity the husband who couldn't keep up with her.

I had feelings for this woman and I didn't know how to tell her. Maybe it was best to be quiet. Maybe after this was over and we got back to Estes Park, when we got back to normal life, things may not be as they were now. We'd been living in a cocoon the past week and with the stress, well, it makes people do things they may otherwise not do. I'd wait till the stress was gone and normalcy returned. We probably wouldn't feel the way we felt now. Life would go on as it had before. *So don't do anything that you'll regret*, I told myself.

The fence was strong and sturdy and I'd just added a foot to its height. It had become a high fence; all weaknesses accounted for and repaired.

Sue made two laps around the park and welcomed the cool

air when she got back into the car.

"Whew, I forgot how the air just beats you down," she said.

"Want a water?" I asked.

"Sure."

I reached behind us, opened the cooler and reached for a bottled water. The ice felt cold but it was melting fast. I gave Sue the bottle and she opened it up, drinking thirstily.

"Are you hungry?" I asked.

She shook her head, finishing the bottle, motioning for another.

Her wish, my command. Right.

I finished my Coke as she drank the second water.

It was three o'clock. I walked to the road, looking my best like a tourist taking a break from his travels. A Mississippi Highway patrol car whizzed by me, headed away from town. Traffic otherwise was country steady: many pickups with beds full of hay or equipment of differing sorts; rigs pulling trailers with horses or pigs; an occasional eighteen-wheeler with cargos of foods and sundries; cattle trucks and county vehicles. A county road crew came along, painting the highway stripes down the middle of the road. The crew consisted of a lead truck carrying a warning sign to oncoming traffic followed by a paint vehicle which automatically sprayed just the right amount of white paint onto the surface of the road. Other than this there was nothing which gave the appearance of what was going to happen tonight at a small Baptist church in rural Mississippi.

At 5:30 Sue and I took the cooler to the table and made our dinner of lunchmeats and chips. We sat like tourists under the maple tree and enjoyed the pleasure of each other's company. I had rolled down the car windows, and kept the ignition on so we could listen to the radio. Muddy Waters' voice poured out as we ate.

Two other vehicles came into the park. One car drove up to the privies. An elderly gentleman got out and used the facilities. His wife was in the front seat. She looked over to us, smiled and waved. Sue waved back. The gentleman came back out, got in the car and away they went. The other vehicle was a pickup with two men inside. I bristled at this sight.

They stopped at the far end of the park away from us. When they got out, I recognized them. So did Sue.

She nudged me, "Those were the two who brought in the generator at the barn the other night."

"I remember them," I whispered. "They set up the interior for the meeting. I had a good look at them then."

The two had a cooler with them and sat at the table to eat. They looked over in our direction. We made certain that our faces were not pointed their way and carried on our own private conversation, acting as common as possible.

Sue asked, "What if they come over?"

"They've never seen us before so there should be no problem. What this does verify is the fact that there is definitely going to be action of some sort tonight."

The two finished eating, used the facilities, ignored us and left, heading west to Bhonson's Corner, no doubt.

It was 7:30 when I became very interested in the road traffic, especially the traffic coming from Old Tchula Road. The day's heat was beginning to cool, the sun going down toward the western horizon. Sue and I moved to a table closer to the road.

The traffic was changing personality. There were more teenaged drivers and families going to or coming from town. Some vehicles had their lights on, some didn't. It wasn't quite sundown but the deep woods seemed to make Mississippi get darker earlier than in other places. I was looking for a red Ford F-150 in particular. I recalled from Jones' speech that he would lead the group to the church. I wanted to see his truck drive by.

It was 8:15 and the sky was darker. A truck was coming along the road from the west. It had only one headlight, on the driver's side, but it was still light enough out to see the red color, the Ford logo and the two figures inside. The passenger was Charlie Goode. I couldn't see the driver clearly, but I was certain it was Jones.

They were looking straight ahead. Sue and I stood and walked away from the road a little, waiting for the parade. Soon another truck came along, and another and another. A sedan followed and another truck behind that. It was steady and it was sinister.

I trotted to the road and watched as the vehicles turned onto Ferguson Road, their engine sounds lost into the trees and hills. I looked at my cell phone and read the time: 8:30.

Sue and I got in the car, pointed it to the highway, and waited.

"I wonder how long it'll take," she said. "I didn't see any police or any sign that authorities are any where around here."

"They're there, to be sure. Jones doesn't know what's waiting for him."

These were serious minutes coming on.

"Do you think they'll put up a fight?" asked Sue.

"I think they're cowards. As soon as they see a power greater than themselves, they'll wilt and pee in their pants and the MBI will cuff them."

"I hope so, or else there could be a terrible consequence."

"I know," I said.

Thirty minutes went by. I wondered what was going on not two miles away. I got out of the car and walked to the road. It was a quiet highway now; only an occasional vehicle passed. I couldn't hear anything coming from deep in the wood behind us, and I, too, wondered what the consequence would be if Jones fought the law. It was pitch black outside. The only sounds were of distant insects and birds.

Then I heard something that didn't belong. It was the whirring of an engine, the sound of a vehicle that was traveling at a high rate of speed, and it was coming from the direction of Ferguson Road.

I walked out onto the road itself to get a better vantage. The sound gradually became distinct and it was getting closer. It was definitely an engine, coming from Ferguson Road, nearing the highway junction.

At first I saw a vague field of light that suddenly became a full headlight spreading at the intersection of Ferguson Road and Highway 12. A pickup truck ran up to the intersection too fast and slowed only to make a turn. The turn was west, and I was standing in the road like a fool.

I ran off the road as the truck weaved and slid its way onto the hard surface, rocking from side to side, skidding, almost losing control on the roadway. I couldn't tell the make but I saw as it headed straight at me that the front passenger headlight was out. It was Jones' truck. It came on and passed the park. I saw the red paint and Jones behind the wheel. He was paying no attention to me, but was intent only on driving.

I jumped into the car.

"It's Jones," I said. "I don't know what's going on, Sue, but I think something went wrong at the church. I'm not going to wait for a posse. Hang on!"

The Chevy didn't disappoint and took to the road quickly. It was no MX-5, but it would do. Jones was a good quarter mile ahead and I pushed the pedal to the metal. I slowed just a fraction at the Old Tchula Road junction, but saw no sign of Jones having turned there. If I was right, he wanted out of this place as quickly as possible. I hit Highway 49 and turned north on a hunch.

When the Chevy was right at 100 mph I saw red tail lights about an eighth of a mile ahead of us. I had to assume it was Jones' truck. The old F-150 wasn't exactly speed-tuned and would be rather easy to catch on a straightaway. If he took to back roads he could lose me. I wouldn't be so familiar as Jones in traveling back roads. He would certainly know someone was chasing him, he just wouldn't know who. He'd likely think it was the law.

I supposed it was the law in a way. A different law, an Old Testament, unforgiving law.

Even at 100 mph I was closing, but not as fast as I had wished. I knew that a dangerous man was in that car ahead so I kept pace with his truck.

We were clocking about ninety-five, headed north on 49 toward Greenwood. Luckily the traffic was practically non-existent. But those other vehicles out on 49 tonight wouldn't have much of a warning when approached from behind.

Sue, buckled in next to me, watched at the intersections for cross traffic. A car came out of a driveway into our lane, and I switched to the other side of the road, only to run at an oncoming truck which was blinking to turn to his left. I took his shoulder and he took the oncoming lane a couple hundred feet before the junction. I vaguely saw the other car go to the ditch to avoid a head-on crash.

My hands were sweating and my nerves were at the surface, ears and eyes alert to all sights and sounds. Our windows were down and the air swept through the interior of the car with a force that whipped our hair and our flesh.

We were closing in on Greenwood, the city lights reflecting off low-hanging clouds, and I was wondering what was going through Jones' head. I didn't have to wait long to find out, because he went straight down Main Street.

We had slowed considerably as we'd come to town. Jones kept on Main and I was following about two blocks behind. Our speeds were just at legal as traffic was steady. I don't even know if Jones knew he was being followed any more. But he wasn't going home, I knew that for sure.

I looked over to Sue. She was as alert as I. She looked at me and smiled briefly.

"You're doing okay," she said.

"Thanks," I said. "It's not the mountain driving I prefer, but it is challenging. I wonder where our friend is headed. I don't think he believes he's being followed any more."

Just then Jones went to Grand Boulevard, heading north of the city. He picked up speed and I did likewise. We went on to C-518, the Money Road.

"He's headed to Cheever's Lumber Mill. I recognize the road," I said.

But Jones had other plans. We passed the mill going better than 85 mph and he continued northbound.

I sped up to get closer. The Illinois Central Railway paralleled our right and a wooded area covered the left, the road curved northerly and we came onto Money. I saw red brake lights shine as Jones slowed down and turned left onto a side street.

FORTY-FIVE

"What the hell?" I said.

I slowed, pulling off the road at the intersection where Jones had turned.

I didn't see him. I stopped the car and listened. There was no sound. Jones had stopped, too.

"Sue, you stay here."

"Rick, no, why?" she protested.

"Take my cell phone and call Jim Harris," I said as I opened the door. "He's in my address book. Tell him where we are. He'll know how to contact MBI. I can't let this scum get away. He's here somewhere. Lock the doors and stay put unless you sense trouble. If you even get the sense of personal danger, drive the hell out of here."

I was out before Sue could argue.

I ran across the road and straight into a wooded lot. In the darkness I had no idea what lay ahead, but I couldn't let Jones escape. My eyes adjusted to the night well enough. Once through the trees, I saw the truck. It was parked off a dirt street in a weedy patch of ground. I ran up to it. The engine hood was hot and steam was rising out of the front grill. Apparently, the truck had run too hot and Jones had ditched it.

So, where the hell was he? I had to assume he knew he was being followed after all, but he wouldn't know by whom. This would bother him. He couldn't judge the type of fight he was in for if he didn't know who was here. But he would be running on a full tank of adrenaline and that posed a real threat. And he might be armed. I didn't know how he'd escaped the MBI, but I had to assume the worst.

My own adrenaline was pumping pretty fast. I was a menace

myself right then, except I was unarmed. I needed to keep that fact in my mind. I looked around and saw only night shapes.

The town was quiet. No one seemed at home. Houses were darkened like the night sky. The moon offered little help except to cast shadows, and to me every shadow looked like a man. I moved to the north and came to a street intersection. To the east was the highway and Sue, one block away. To the west was virtually the end of the town and the Tallahatchie River.

Just east of where I stood, there was an abandoned building. It was a two-story wooden framed structure that had seen better days. Broken windows, from what I could see, the rear door hanging on its hinges, roof partially caved in. A perfect place to hide?

I crouched and ran to the building and took residence beneath a window. Leaning my back against the siding and kneeling toward the ground, I moved upward, the left side of my face rubbing against the weather-roughened siding to the window frame. Cautiously, I looked inside.

A small room lay quiet with the night and I could vaguely see the side opposite from the window in the murky dark. I moved to the door and stretched my left leg up over the uncertain steps onto the door sill. I grabbed the inside frame on either side of the door and gently lifted myself into the building. With my back momentarily silhouetted against the open night, I was a target.

I dropped down to my hands and knees and felt my way to the right, where I found a doorway opening to what appeared to be a much larger room. At one time this had been a place of business. A staircase led up to the second level. I bypassed this and focused on the front part of the building. I also listened. There was no sound anywhere. I remained quiet and listened more deeply. If Jones was here, I was certain I'd hear him breathe. There was nothing.

Something in me knew, however, that he was in there. And he knew he wasn't alone. A minute went by without a sound. It appeared to be a stalemate. My eyes had adjusted to the dark as much as they could, and I knew there was one way to get a rise out of Jones. If he wasn't in here, I'd lose a little pride, but if he was here, then it would soon be over, one way or the other. What light there was dimly outlined various shapes. I remembered something I'd once read: "It was a dead place now, this place of the gods."

There were what looked like three aisles of shelving. At one time this shell of a building had been a dry goods store or a clothing store, perhaps. To my left, a counter ran the length of the northern wall and beyond the counter was the front entrance. It was bordered by two windows on either side, now glass-empty and sloppily boarded up.

I crouched deeply, hands on the floor and toes on end and in one movement, with a wild yell, leaped full body into the room, falling and rolling toward the counter.

Instantly a shot rang out. No question as to who'd pulled the trigger. The bullet struck the floor beside me, splintering wood onto my left arm. I didn't wonder about weapons any more. I continued to roll and found my feet when Jones tried once again. Another shot rang out loudly and close. My ears echoed with the sound and I lost my balance for a bit, but he missed. This bullet plowed deeply into the door frame. As soon as I heard the sound and got my balance, I jumped to my feet and took the chance that I would see Jones and be able to beat his next shot.

I was up and facing the counter. He stood behind it and, thank God, he must have had a single shot revolver, because he was cocking as I hurled my full weight over the counter top and into his midsection. As I hit him he had one more chance at me and took it, but the gun clicked empty. We hit the wall behind the counter and both went down, me on top with both arms tight around his middle. He had lost his breath momentarily. I heard the rush of air escape the lungs as we hit the floor.

He still had his gun in his right hand. He bounced it off my head repeatedly till I had to let go out of self-preservation. Jones found his breath again and freed himself from me. He was up before I could move to position, and he started kicking me, cussing the whole time.

"Ya sum' bitch. I'll kick yer fuckin' head to mush! Goddamn whoever ya are!"

He was a good kicker. His shoes were steel-toed and doing their job. I covered my head with my hands and arms the best I could, but there was no let-up in the bastard. I had to get out of the way and had to do it now.

I rolled again, but toward Jones instead of away from him, lifting my legs and crossing them at his knees, scissoring his legs hard till he went down against the counter. I freed my legs, stood, and put my right shoulder into his midsection again, wrapped my arms around his chest and lifted. Jones went up but his gun and fists began again knocking against my head and back. I didn't feel a thing. I was intent on only one outcome here.

I was in full football mode, and there was about to be one hell of a tackle coming up. With Jones pounding my head all the while, I ran him right into the boarded-up front window of the building, breaking through, over the sill and onto the front porch, my shoulder placed squarely into his diaphragm. Down we went together and turned over each other, rolling off the porch onto the front landing and onto what used to be a sidewalk.

Jones was hurting. The blows to my head were less intense than they had been. The gun had flown out of his hand with the tackle, but he was still kicking hard and planted one in my crotch. I lost my breath just long enough for him to get free from my grasp.

He was up. He ran to the Chevy and tried to get in, but Sue had locked the doors. Jones looked my way and saw me coming.

He shouted, "Who the fuck are you anyway?"

I was five feet from him, face to face, on the other side of the car. "I'm here to wipe your white ass. Do you want fries with that, you bastard?"

He looked at me like he didn't quite get it. He gave Sue a questioning glance through the window, turned and sprinted toward the railroad tracks just beyond the car. He tried hopping over them but got caught up on the second rail, tripping over and falling onto the graveled soil on the other side.

I came right behind, taking the tracks in one leap and was on him again. The fight wasn't in Jones like it had been before, but he was sinewy and tried weaseling out from under my weight. He squirmed enough to get to his hands and knees. My grip fell to his ankles and he kicked hard. That freed him again. I looked up just in time to take a full force kick into my face. I felt my nose collapse. If he had known how accurate he'd been with that kick he could have finished the job right there, but he was more interested in running. He went into the shrubbery on the other side of the tracks.

I recovered, wiping blood from my broken nose.

Jones didn't know how to run with class. He was all arms and legs, like the Oz scarecrow, plowing deeper into the grasses of an open field. I had him in twenty seconds, tackling him at his ankles. Jones went face down into the soft dirt of the field. He turned over to start kicking again. I stood and fended off his kicks with my arms.

"You little weasel," I yelled. "Stop kicking!"

He stopped kicking, surprising me because I was rather looking forward to the fight.

I stared down at him. Jones' hands went to his face and he screamed. This looked like a trick, so I backed up a few feet to get ready for whatever he had planned next. But Jones continued to scream. His hands were frantically brushing at his face and arms. I stepped cautiously toward him and saw what had his attention.

When he'd fallen, Jones had landed on a fire ant hill and those little soldiers were quite unhappy about it. He continued to flail at his face, his neck, and his arms.

"Get up, you son-of-a-bitch." I was not to be denied.

He started wheezing, his eyes wide open. He tried talking but only gasps came out. He was in misery. I leaned down to look at his face. The ants were quite industrious. I reached down to his legs and dragged him away from the nest.

"My inhaler, my inhaler," his voice rasped.

He was working to breathe. His inhaler? I recalled an antihistamine inhaler Sue and I'd found in Jones' house the day we searched it. Jones was allergic to the venom of the red ant and he was reacting.

Then I heard the crush of shoes on gravel coming up behind me.

"Rick, where's Jones?" Sue asked, running toward me.

"At supper." I looked over my shoulder at her.

"Supper?"

"Not where he eats, but where *he* is eaten."

Sue was beside me and she looked down at Jones, who was still struggling at every breath, his eyes out of focus, imploring us for help.

There was no help. I had nothing for treatment, but I did have something to say.

I leaned close to his ears and said, "I can't help you. You are going to die, Sam Jones. This task is just about finished."

He stared, the ants continuing their defense.

But Jones didn't hear me; he wasn't seeing anything any more. His eyes looked blankly out into the night sky, mouth wide open, no more gasps for air.

I turned to Sue, took her by her arms and made her look away.

"He's really dead?" she asked.

"Not dead enough."

"Was there anything we could have done?"

"No," I said. "Jones was allergic and full of venom. It's over."

"When I heard the gunfire, I thought you were hurt or worse."

"I'm okay," I said.

She leaned in, wrapping her arms tightly around me. I held her close and felt her hair in my face. Her body was shaking. She pushed away slowly and looked in my eyes. "I was afraid he'd killed you."

"Didn't happen."

Sue let go her grasp, taking one last look at the dead man and turned back toward the car. I followed her example and looked at Sam Jones. What a little man to have caused such pain and misery to others.

I caught up to Sue. "Did you get Jim Harris?"

"Yes," she said. "He contacted the MBI, and they called your cell phone to verify. They should be here any minute."

"We can find out what went wrong at the church tonight."

I held Sue's hand as we got to the car and she leaned her head against my shoulder. I opened the door for her and she got in. I walked to the other side but before getting in, I looked across the road at the building where Jones and I had fought. A sad smile came to me. The broken structure was the old grocery where

Emmett Till had walked into history so long ago, the symbol for where the struggle began. And now, in its own disrepair and perhaps final gasp of life, that old hatred had perhaps turned on itself.

But maybe not. I recalled a poem from years ago, and it seemed fitting in all this.

> *In the desert*
> *I saw a creature, naked, bestial.*
> *Who, squatting upon the ground,*
> *Held his heart in his hands,*
> *And ate of it.*
> *I said, "Is it good, friend?"*
> *"It is bitter – bitter", he answered.*
> *"But I like it*
> *Because it is bitter,*
> *And because it is my heart."*

I stayed there for a while, by the door of the car, gazing at that old building. I imagined ghostly images of happy black and white children running into that very store for candied treats and coming back out to play their innocent games of checkers and hide-and-seek, free from those fears where man feeds on his own bile of racial hatred. I turned my gaze to the road that ran past Money, to the Mississippi trees above, to the stars beyond, and I said a little prayer for us all.

FORTY-SIX

Sirens cried out and many vehicles arrived in Money that night.

Agent Smithland was first out of the lead car. He saw me and didn't look so happy. "So, you don't understand English very well," he snarled. "Stay put meant *stay put*."

I shrugged. "Well, Agent Smithland, I did say I wouldn't intrude. I didn't say I'd stay put."

"But you did intrude when you started the chase."

"Whoops, I lied." I turned to Sue. "I have sinned. Three Our Fathers and three Hail Marys?"

"You're not Catholic, Rick."

"Ma'am, I am tonight."

As I walked Agent Smithland over to Jones I explained the allergic reaction. He simply confirmed what I already knew—Jones was dead. He wasn't going to hurt anyone ever again.

I asked Smithland about the events at the church and about what went wrong.

"The MBI let Jones and his crew start the fires, which were quickly put out by agents prepared with foam sprayers and water," he told me. "Most of the men quit as soon as they saw MBI agents on the outside pinching them in from 360 degrees. He said that Jones gave up also, but when agents went to confront him, Jones reached down to a hidden ankle holster, pulled out a pistol and took our best agent, Harlan Richert, hostage."

Smithland went on. "With a gun to his head, Jones took Richert to his truck, unlocked the door and pushed him in through the driver's side. Jones headed back to Highway 12. We gave pursuit, but before we got two miles from the church, we discovered Agent Richert lying alongside the road. He was unconscious. You don't leave an agent like that. We radioed for local assistance, giving the truck description. We didn't know which way Jones had turned at the highway."

"That's when I took action," I said. "Sue and I had found a spot to observe the goings-on of the night. When we saw Jones, we realized something went wrong, so we went after him till his truck gave up the fight."

I explained what happened after that.

Smithland seem relieved. He said that we would have to be officially interviewed and fill out a report tomorrow afternoon. Smithland himself would be at the motel at noon to take both our statement of events and assist in writing the report.

"Because of you, Mr. Burns, Parchman will have to add a new wing to the farm," he said. "Not bad for a Yank, and a white Yank at that." He laughed for the first time and added, "FTNF has ceased to exist as of tonight, and that's given me great personal pleasure. Thank you, Mr. Burns."

"Call me Rick," I said. "And you're welcome."

We shook hands. It was over. Sue and I got into the car and left.

"Well, Rick, we did it," she said as we drove back to Greenwood.

I looked over to her and smiled. "Yah, FTNF is done, kaput. I'm saddened and relieved both. Bob and Amy did not have to die, but they did die. Their deaths are avenged, and I don't care what they say, revenge definitely has its place."

We were tired . . . too tired to eat. Thanks to Sam Jones I had pains in places I didn't realize could hurt. The nose would heal itself.

We went to our rooms. A few minutes later I was in the shower, the hot water beating on my aching bones, and a few minutes after that I was in bed. I don't remember my head hitting the pillow.

The morning came. I was up and turned on CNN right away. They had the story from last night as a 'just in' segment. I threw on a pair of shorts and my Salty Dog tee. Sue knocked at my door just before noon. She likewise had on shorts and was wearing a blue tank top.

No sooner was she inside than Agent Smithland knocked. We gave an official statement and were filling out the report when I mentioned the CNN story. He said that our names would be kept out of the press for as long as possible, but that there would be no escaping the fifteen minutes of fame coming our way.

After he left, I turned to Sue and said, "How would you like to eat really well tonight?"

"As I haven't eaten since yesterday afternoon, 'really well' sounds really good to me."

"I brought a good shirt along but I need another pair of pants."

"I need a few things myself. Let's go shopping."

There was a sparkle in her eyes when she said 'shopping' that scared me just a little.

We went downtown and split up, Sue to the ladies store and I to the men's store. After I had finished with my shopping, while waiting for Sue, I found a tobacconist who believed in the sanctity of walk-in humidors. There I found a quiet refuge, enjoying the varied aromas, and I also found an Ashton Classic that would go perfectly with an after dinner Fonseca cognac. Or a beer . . . whatever.

I met Sue at the car. She had a large bag filled with goodies but wouldn't share the contents.

Again, we went to our rooms. At 8:00 I was ready to eat. I had bought a pair of khaki gabardine trousers. As I was changing I noticed a large bruise on my left thigh where one of Jones' kicks had punished especially well. It was quite tender to the touch but the smooth fabric of the pants felt like a relieving massage. I'd also bought shoes: penny loafers with class. My white and blue striped long-sleeved shirt completed the set. I was going to knock Sue dead with my mannish good looks.

I knocked at Sue's door. When she opened it, it was I who was knocked dead. She was wearing a fitted v-neck, very little black dress. I stared. I know I looked the fool. She was stunning. The dress had an off-center slit, and it was accessorized with black sandals and a silver toned necklace and earring set with dangling colored beads. The necklace fell just above the 'v' of her dress. The earrings were two inches long, emphasizing her already long and graceful figure. She looked elegant, and I suddenly wasn't so hungry any more.

"I'm starved," she said.

"Me too," I lied.

"Where are we going?"

"Well, Jim Bob at the front desk suggested Giardina's, downtown."

"Sounds wonderful," she said.

Five minutes later we were at the restaurant. Inside, we were escorted to a table by a young lady who seemed especially courteous. If was quite nice.

We started with appetizers. I had a cup of crawfish bisque and Sue had a crabmeat cocktail. Watching her eat was different now than it had been during the last several days. She ate slowly, seemingly enjoying each bite, each portion, while I bullied my crawfish like a dog.

For the main course, I had a porterhouse, rare, thank you very much, with sautéed mushrooms. Sue had the veal Piccata with a side of grilled asparagus, an excellent choice. A bottle of Kendall-Jackson Cabernet Sauvignon was good to go with the entrée. It's a still wine and God knew I needed 'still' at this meal.

We ate for an hour. Even as I ate, I couldn't take my eyes from Sue. She seemed shy in comparison. I wondered if she knew how I felt or even cared how I felt.

It was already hitting both of us. This was the end of the odyssey and, as I had imagined, things would be different. I wondered *how* things would be different.

"Speaking of next fall, are you going to sign your contract?" she asked.

I didn't recall that we had been speaking of next fall.

"As soon as we get back," I said.

"And why are you going to sign your contract?"

"Because I will know what to do with the next Josh Holston that comes along. I won't run away from the responsibility."

"And you think you can do that in the classroom?"

"I know I can, and with my wing-man there for back-up, how

can I fail?"

"That's the man I know. By the way, it's wing-woman."

When we were finished eating, I passed on the cognac and cigar. Somehow, it didn't feel right anymore. There were other things to do. I paid for this meal. Sue didn't fight it.

It was dark outside, a whole different kind of dark than it had been just twenty-four hours ago. And it had started to rain.

We hurried to the car. The air was cool by Mississippi standards. I turned on the engine and the wipers, watching the steady back and forth motion of the blades pushing water to either side of the windshield. I watched the rainwater spanking the hood and beading there. Sue sat quietly beside me.

The drive back to the motel . . . leisurely and smooth.

"You looked to be out of shape last night, Mr. Burns," she said, turning her body toward me after a minute of silent communication. "Breathing a little too hard, I'd say."

"Pardon me, Miss Richy?"

"You heard me."

"I'll have you know that I'm in better shape than you might think. I run twenty laps around the school track three or four times a week in the summer."

"Twenty laps. Is that on the grown-up track?" The corners of her mouth twitched. "I'm impressed. How do you keep count of twenty laps? It must take you an hour to run that far. I'd think you would forget your lap count after maybe two or three laps. That's a big number for someone like you, isn't it?"

So this is the game she wanted to play. I can give as well as I can take. We pulled into the motel, under the canopied front entryway, protected from the steady rain. I stopped the car, put it in park and looked at Sue.

"For your information, as I run the laps, I keep count on my fingers. After I reach ten, why then I keep count on my toes."

Sue's eyebrows rose considerably. I looked at the windshield and continued. "However, as a result of a farm accident when I was a young lad, I lost one of my toes, leaving only nine. I can never quite get that last lap counted for certain."

At this, I side-glanced at Sue a look of victory, got out of the car and walked around to her door. I opened it for her and reached in for her hand. She obliged, moving legs-first to the pavement, rising to meet me face-to-face.

"Just add one to nine," she whispered.

"Oh, I suppose that might work."

Her body leaned against mine. She raised her arms up to and wrapped them around my neck. "I love you," she said, her voice soft and gentle.

I could feel her breath on my lips. The fence crumbled. Oh shit.

I took her face in my hands. I leaned slightly down to her, and when our lips met all the drifted snows of uncertainties melted. Her flesh became my flesh. My arms enveloped her completely and wholly. Sue pressed against me, and I felt an energy flow, electrically charged and even a little bit dangerous. I was dizzy from the passion of it.

When we finally pulled away from each other, there was no doubt in my mind what the future held. We walked through the motel entrance, both of Sue's arms wrapped around my left arm, her head on my shoulder, a smile on her lips.

We walked up to the front desk. Jim Bob was there.

"Can I help y'all tonight, Mr. Burns?"

"Jim Bob, my fine southern friend. I want to cancel my two rooms. Is that possible?"

"Yes sir, for you it is, sir. Are y'all leaving us tonight?"

"Oh, no, not at all Jim Bob."

"Sir?"

I looked at Sue. She looked content, turning her gaze to the young man with two first names.

"Give me one room, your best, one bed, one night, for two," I said.

THE END

Made in the USA
Charleston, SC
13 April 2010